THE REBELLIOUS RED

THE RAVISHING REES #4

ROSAMUND WINCHESTER

THE RAVISHING REES
GANWYD O'R MOR

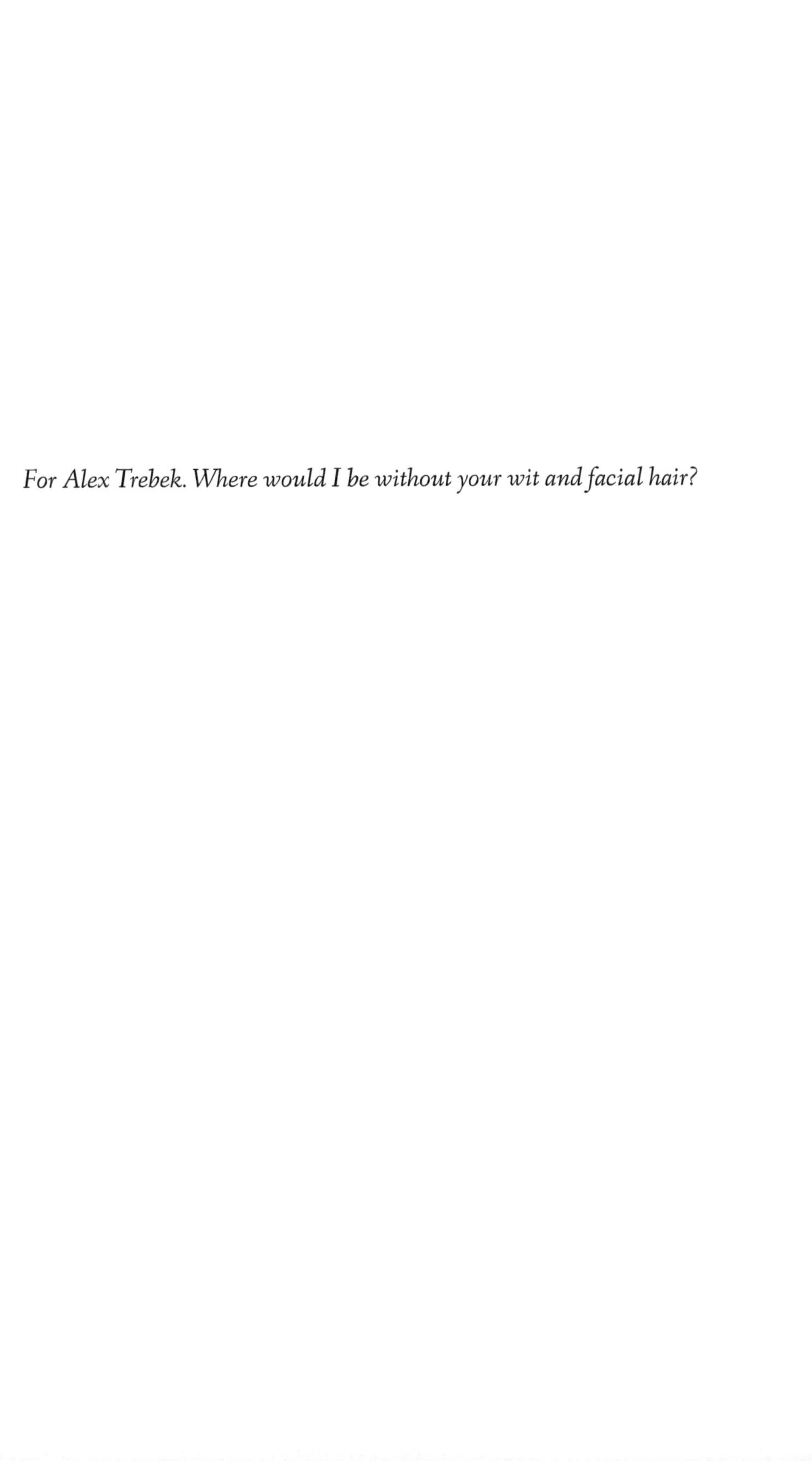

For Alex Trebek. Where would I be without your wit and facial hair?

PROLOGUE

The Heather Bell
Off the coast of Wales
1424 A.D.

It was the silence she noticed first...and then the stillness. It seemed that, though the sun had risen from its slumber, neither the wind nor the sea herself had been roused from their beds.

But neither the silence nor the stillness lasted all that long.

"Rose, love, get back down below decks! 'Tis too dangerous up here!" her father yelled; his usually booming voice barely audible through the angry screaming of the storm. The waves battered the ship, lifting it and throwing it as if it were a mere toy, and they were growing tired of playing with it.

The ship pitched violently, and she gasped, her mind echoing with the sounds of her pounding heart.

What am I doin'? What did I come up here for?

Just after dawn, she'd clamored on deck, seeking her papa out.

She'd had a restless night, the swelling and abating of the sea a jarring lullaby. Her mama hadn't slept well, either, but she'd remained below decks in their small shared cabin, the one they'd purchased for the long voyage from Scotland to Wales.

Once on deck, the violent orange and purple painting the horizon stole her attention, the colors a vivid contrast to the dark, ominous gray billowing along to collide with it.

A storm.

Arriving as quickly as it had appeared, she watched the storm stalk them. She stood, frozen in place, her bare toes curling, almost as if she could find purchase on the wooden planks beneath her feet.

A yell split the air, shocking her from her thoughts, and her focus was immediately recaptured by the sight of her father, her darling papa, struggling to make his way to where she was pressed against the mast, her thin arms wrapped around it as if to embrace it. Her papa's large frame was hunched against the wind, his usually bright red hair black from the inundation of water pouring over the side of the ship.

"Rose! Get below! Now!" her papa's voice was all but snatched away by a gust of wind. But she'd heard him. She knew what he wanted her to do, and she knew she had to do it, but her feet remained affixed to the deck, her heart thundering, her chest tight.

That soon changed, though, when another wave crashed against the starboard side. Her small body flew sideways, slamming into the deck and sliding until she hit the railing on the leeward side.

"Rose!" her papa screamed. Stunned by the impact, she failed to raise her head. She blinked, the water in her face plastering the lengths of her hair to her cheeks and eyelashes.

"Papa," she squeaked, attempting to rise.

He was there in an instant, his strong arms easily lifting her, though her legs fought to hold her upright.

"Darlin', ye need tae go tae yer mother," her papa rasped against her ear. "I dinnae want ye up here. 'Tisn't safe fer ye—"

His words were cut off by a loud crack as the ship heaved to the side, nearly sending all on the deck into the water. Around her, men were scrambling to secure the rigging and themselves. Shouts mingled with the claps of thunder and the crashing of the waves, a cacophony of the sea god's music.

Trembling, her body chilled to the bone, Rose curled into her papa's chest, the fleeting warmth of his embrace a miniscule comfort, for all the world around her was tumbling.

Another crack shook the ship. The rope holding the barrels of lamp oil secure snapped, and the barrel in front rolled free just as the ship heaved, sending the barrel into the air. When the barrel smashed into the deck, everything went terribly wrong.

The oil spread quickly, making the already perilous deck that much more dangerous. The wooden planks beneath her bare feet were slick.

She lost her footing. Her father lost his hold.

He screamed, the sound of terror snatched up by the gale.

She tumbled backward over the railing, her thin arms flailing uselessly. The water caught her, then immediately devoured her.

The world went quiet. It grew dark behind her eyes.

CHAPTER 1

The Bearded Lady
Port Eynon Bay, Wales
1446 A.D.

"Goddamn, woman! How the hell did ye do that?" the scowling man bellowed, his purplish-red face pock-marked, his wide eyes unfocused as he stared down at his mate, unconscious on the floor beneath the table.

She shrugged. "When they tell tales of me, they do not exaggerate—you should have known that, Wickey," she drawled, her words perfectly pronounced even though she'd just thrown back her tenth shot of whiskey.

She'd woken with a taste for whiskey, had stumbled down the stairs from her room and into the pub, and had gratified her thirst. Too bad she couldn't do it in peace, not with two of the three ship crews puttering around town, looking for pleasure and trouble, and sometimes those things were the same.

Wickey, the old goat, sneered, his front teeth missing.

"So yer a mermaid, then, with swords fer tits, and a quim made of solid gold." He stuck out his chest, crossing his arms and raising his chin, taunting her. The old bastard.

She gasped, pressing a hand to her neck in feigned shock. "Who told you that?" she asked sharply.

Chuckling to himself—a sound very much like a ship's hull scraping against a sandbar—Wickey glanced at the crowd that had gathered for the drinking contest, his grin big.

"Ye mean 'tisn't true, then?" he asked, his lips curling into another sneer. He thought he had her, the fool.

Rose almost rolled her eyes. Instead, she shrugged, casting Wickey a bored expression, one she'd perfected over the years. "Nay, I only asked so that I could thank the man *properly*. God doesn't give a woman a golden quim without expecting her to use it."

The crowd erupted into guffaws and Rose leaned back in her chair, winking at Wickey whose face was doing an atrocious imitation of a roasted fish. Red, bloated, and with protruding eyes.

Blubbering, Wickey picked up a tankard and tossed it across the room, narrowly missing Burgess, the bar keep.

"Oi, ye git!" Burgess bellowed, making everyone in the bar flinch, except Rose, of course. She knew Burgess was all bark and some growling, but he didn't bite. Often.

"Come now, Burgess," Rose called, "he's only mad that my *swords* are bigger than his."

Again, the crowd erupted, the laughter making the few other bar occupants turn to stare from their corner table. There were two of them, rough looking men, their beards as thick as their necks.

Rose had noticed them when she'd come downstairs. She noticed everything. It was part of what made her such a damn good "whisperer"; the one Rees tasked with listening at keyholes, hiding in shadows, and sharing all the juicy bits she uncovered with her cousin, Saban, the Brenin—King—of their family business.

Smuggling. And occasionally piracy. And sometimes murder. But never of the innocent.

The men in the corner continued their murmured conversation, but their gazes remained on her, their expressions unreadable. She mentally shrugged; she didn't care what they were talking about or why they were looking at her. If they were in Port Eynon Bay, in the Bearded Lady, they knew her family, they knew *her*, and they knew better than to piss in her drink.

Picking up the nearly empty tumbler in front of her, she threw back the last of the whiskey, the burn like a tickle in her throat.

His face redder than the kerchief around his bloated neck, Wickey turned tail and lumbered from the room, leaving his mate on the floor, under the table. The soused man was groaning in his stupor, and Rose wanted to laugh about it. But the laughter wouldn't come, not real laughter, only the forced laughter. True merriment had fled her soul long ago.

Sighing, she waved off the remaining crowd with a single movement of her arm, clearing the area around her table. Leaving her in peace.

Peace? She snorted.

Leaning back in her chair, she caught sight of one of the unknown men tipping his chin in her direction, a glint of curiosity in his dark eyes.

For the first time that day, she allowed her own curiosity to lead her, pushing her chair back and standing. Without hesitation, she strode to the corner, stopping just before their table. She stared down at them, they stared up at her, and the man on the right's gaze flicked down to her breasts.

Hell, he wasn't the first one to do that, but something about what he was doing felt...strange.

Unthinkingly, she slid her fingers up over the golden locket which was cradled in the crease of her bosom, the golden chain from which it dangled snagged in the wisps of red hair that had come loose from her braid.

Drawing herself up to her full height—which was not much taller than the underbelly of a sixteen-hand horse, she let the man look his fill. The man on the other side of the table pursed his lips, his gaze flicking between his friend and Rose.

"Is there something you want from me, stranger?" she finally asked, her voice clearer than you'd think it would be after a full bottle of Scotch whiskey.

The man's lips quirked.

"Aye, I might," he answered, his Scottish brogue easy to recognize.

Disbelief made her lips curl, and she crossed her arms, making her breasts all the more prominent. When she dragged herself from her bed, she hadn't cared that her shirt was the same one she'd worn over the last week, or that the buttons meant to secure the thing all the way up to her neck were unfastened to just between where her breasts met her abdomen. For some reason, the urge to pull the shirt closed prodded her, but she stabbed it, unwilling to change anything about anything right in that moment.

It took too much energy...and she had to care enough. Which she didn't.

"What do you think I can give you? Unlike my cousins, I don't like giving away what I can sell. For outrageous amounts." A smile tilted her lips.

The men both chuckled, but the one of the right stopped quickly, his gaze, once again, falling on her breasts. No. Not her breasts, the locket. The one thing from her hazy past that her grandfather told her to keep. It had been a part of her memory for as long as she could remember, and that first thing she could remember was waking up on the beach, a dark-haired man staring down at her, his large hand cupping her face with a gentleness that didn't match the cold glinting in his sea green eyes.

Grasping the locket between her fingers she glowered at the man.

"You won't be having this, if that is what you're after," she practically growled.

The man raised his hands as if to show her he meant no harm. She snorted. Better than anyone, she knew harm came in all forms.

It was why she'd never allowed herself a moment's calm. Or peace.

"I dinnae want yer bauble, lass, I only mean that I want tae know more 'bout where ye got it," the man remarked, dropping his hands to wrap them around his completely full tankard.

Narrowing her eyes, she answered, "I've always had it."

The man took her answer and swallowed, his expression thoughtful.

"Do ye know where ye got it?" he asked, and she realized she was actually answering the man rather than placing a knife-point at his throat.

"My parents," she answered. Her parents...two people whose faces and names she couldn't even conjure in her mind. "'Tis the only thing I have from them." She swallowed down the circling sorrow, knowing it would offer nothing but darkness. "Why?"

The man eyed her, his dark gaze taking in all that Rose allowed others to see. And, once again, his gaze dropped to her locket.

"What if I told ye somethin' ye dinnae know 'bout that bit o' gold 'round yer neck?"

She shrugged, using every bit of her self-control to keep from wrapping her fingers around the man's neck.

"You can say what you want, stranger. I won't pay you a shilling." She wouldn't part with her hard-earned money for all the information in the world. Her gold was the only thing she could count on.

What about the Rees? She shut off those thoughts with brutal precision. The Rees weren't her blood, but they were more family than any blood relation she could remember, which was one single person: a father she only remembered in the moments before waking.

"I dinnae want yer money, lass..." the man replied, his large hands rubbing at his chin.

"Then what do you want?"

"Nary a thing, lass. Naught but tae reunite a family...." The man stopped talking, and it felt as though the very breath in her chest froze, filling her body with ice and foreboding and fear.

Fear was no better than remorse. It was useless. A weakness.

I am never weak.

"What do you mean, stranger?" Aye, what did he mean?

The man's lips quirked once more.

"I've seen that image before, lass. The rose wound 'round the thorn. 'Tis the crest o' a clan far north o' here."

A clan in the north?

"Scotland?" she asked, her heart pounding—and she didn't know why.

The man nodded. "Aye."

Rose looked down even as she lifted the locket from her cleavage for her own inspection. A rose, its stem twined around a thorn, the sharp end pointed directly at her heart.

Suddenly, her body was heavy, the blood in her veins like lead. Her mind, her heart, her very soul, told her that moment was a break in the road, one that lead in one direction and the other, another.

But which one to take?

Swallowing her fear—that useless emotion—she drawled, "Tell me what you know."

CHAPTER 2

Gleneden Castle
Home of the Laird MacPherson
Kinloch Rannoch, Scotland

Dubhach "Thorn" MacPherson barely noticed the door to his study slamming shut as another lying schemer hurried away in a snit. As with the other women he'd vetted and dismissed over the last four years, since returning to Scotland, the woman had begged him to give her the chance to prove that she was who she said she was. There was no need for a second chance, though, and he'd told her so.

They never got what they wanted...because he never got what he wanted.

A grin curled his lips as he finished straightening his tartan. The pleats were perfect, though he still smoothed them with his hands. He didn't know why, but since that morning, there had been an unruly nervousness suffusing his body. He couldn't sit still, he couldn't focus on any one thing, and he felt the overwhelming need to get on his horse and ride to the loch.

Of course, as the laird, he couldn't just leave, jaunting off to do whatever he wanted. He had a responsibility to his people, a responsibility that he took as seriously as death.

Striding to the table beside the immense stone hearth, Thorn poured himself a sizeable amount of whiskey, raising the tumbler to his lips. The scent of it burned his nostrils, and he welcomed the burn. It was one of the few things lately that could clear the fog from his head. A fog he'd been fighting off since his father's death.

Sighing, Thorn eased his large frame into his oak and leather seat, kicking his feet out and stretching his long, thick legs out before him. The heat of the blazing fire warmed the soles of his feet, drawing the tension from him.

At least for a short while.

A loud knock on the door made him turn, calling for the blackguard to enter.

His best friend and the biggest pain in his arse pushed the door open, stepping inside. He closed the door behind him and strode to where Thorn was lounging.

"There was another one," Garrick drawled, dropping into the high-backed chair on the other side of the hearth. He kicked his feet up, planting them on the pile of wood, and leaning back to peer at Thorn contemplatively. "We sent her on her way."

Thorn nodded, sighing, before leaning back in his own chair. Flexing his long, thick legs out before him, he took another gulp of whiskey, appreciating the burn as it slid over his tongue, down his throat, and into the hollow place in his chest.

"Why didn't you summon me?" Thorn asked, tipping his head to watch his friend's expressions. For a man as brutal as Garrick was in battle, the fool couldn't hide his thoughts worth a piss.

Garrick sniffed. "Ye were already busy with the other lass, dinnae think ye'd be up tae it."

Thorn chuckled humorlessly. "Then you know me well, man.

One a week is enough, but they are coming two to three every seven days now. 'Tis like they are crawling from a pit in the earth where schemers are grown."

Garrick arched an eyebrow, his lips thinning. Thorn knew the man disliked dealing with the flood of women who'd come to Gleneden over the last four years, but Garrick wasn't the one who had to wade through the thickening sludge of women who'd come to his threshold, begging for an audience with him, only to tell him lies.

"Are ye no' tired of it?" Garrick asked, and Thorn chuckled again.

"These women come here to lay claim to something they have no right to, lying to my face about who they are. Of course I am tired of it, but what choice do I have?" Aye, what could he do? Since his fourteenth year, he'd been promised to marry—a contract written, signed, and sealed between his father and his father's closest friend. He'd been a mere lad when he'd first set eyes on the babe he would one day marry. "Ye are bound tae her, lad. And I have sworn tae her da that ye will make a wife o' her and ye will protect her..." He could so easily remember his father's commission: marry, protect.

And I will not fail him.

What did it matter that his betrothed had fallen overboard during a shipwreck or that she hadn't been heard from in twenty-one years. He knew she'd survived—another survivor had helped her ashore before he'd fallen unconscious and lost sight of her—but he had no idea where to begin looking for her.

And what a fool he'd been to ask for help finding her. Now, there were young women pounding on his door at all hours, seeking him out to tell him they were who he'd been searching for.

Liars, the lot of them. Thankfully, it was easy enough to disprove their claims, but with every one sent on their way, another weight pressed down on his shoulders.

"How many more do ye think will come?" Garrick asked, his shoulders drooping in fatigue.

Suddenly, the weight pushed on him, squeezing a grunt from his chest. He closed his eyes, the burn of frustration behind his lids.

"I am seeking my long-lost betrothed..." It had begun as a way to include his people in his search for the woman he was determined to marry. But, it had degenerated into something he couldn't have possibly expected.

He grunted again at the memory. His own bloody idiocy had utterly buggered him. He'd been a fool to think that he, a wealthy laird, could embark on his search for a wife and not have women eager for wealth and security see it as a challenge.

"What if ye married someone ye know?" Garrick broke the tense silence, making Thorn's head snap up.

"You mean for me to marry your sister?" Thorn didn't like what Garrick was suggesting.

A look of horror passed over Garrick's face. So, not his sister, Marbeth, then.

"Ye, yerself, said that Briar is a fine lass, and she has been pinin' after ye since she was nae taller than her da's knee."

Briar MacPherson, with the long black hair, striking dark eyes, and curvy hips. Aye, he'd noticed her every once in a while, especially when she was throwing herself at him in those quiet moments when she could get him alone. So far, he'd fended her off, thinking she was more a distraction than a solution.

"You mean that I would marry Briar to finally end the nightmare of turning away countless lasses who lie to my face at every opportunity?" Would that be so difficult, to marry, end the parade of schemers, and find some peace?

Nay! Briar wasn't the woman he'd been promised to marry. His father had practically written that marriage contract with his own blood...but his father was dead, and so was the man he'd sworn to.

"I can smell yer thoughts from here, *braithair*," Garrick remarked, his nose scrunched up as if he'd scented something repugnant. "Briar is a MacPherson, she will tend ye well. And then, ye could end the parade o' tarts that have been turnin' the castle intae a fair o' horrors."

Marry to end it all. His body stiffened as the thoughts sank deep. It could work. Even as the voice crying out to honor his father rose, he silenced it. It was possible that, after twenty-one years, the lass he was promised to wed was already dead. Was it fair to him, to the future of his clan, to wait for someone who would never come, to search for someone he'd never find?

Garrick's eyes narrowed as if in consideration. "T'would have tae be a quick engagement, otherwise they will continue tae come, poundin' on the door."

Thorn nodded, a smile slowly spreading over his face.

Tapping his chin in thought, Thorn considered Briar. She was a lovely, buxom wench, the daughter of his father's second cousin. She'd been raised in the castle after her father died at war with the MacDougals more than twenty years ago. Since his return, she'd acted as the chatelaine, and while she'd run the castle with swift and exacting efficiency, she wasn't so skilled at hiding her jealousy. Every time a new "betrothed" came knocking, Briar's dark eyes would glitter, her lips would thin, and she'd always be underfoot. In the beginning, he'd found it somewhat humorous, because he'd never considered her more than the daughter of a cousin. But, as the years wore on, he'd become inured to her antics.

And now you are considering marrying the woman.

She was lovely enough, already knew how to run his household... would it really be so difficult to bed her? To beget bairns with her?

Sighing, he let the thoughts and questions stir in his mind until, finally, he said, "I will think on it. In the meantime, secure the castle gates. I am not in the mood for another night of fending off pretenders."

Garrick snapped a nod and departed.

Left alone once more, Thorn retreated to his bed, lying down to stare up into the familiar ceiling overhead.

"What if I make the wrong decision?" Just then, his mind surged with worries. What would his people think if he married someone other than the woman his father had bound him to all those years ago.

Surely, they will understand. Little Rosette MacDeargh had been lost long ago, and the chances of her having survived on her own for so long were.... He shuddered, once again feeling the prick of guilt at the thought of her tragic death. She and her family had been on their way to Wales, to him, when their ship had gone down.

If that man were right, and he had pulled Rosette from the sea, there was always the slim chance that she could be found, that she could find her way home to Gleneden.

Swearing, Thorn realized that he'd never been one to leave much to chance.

CHAPTER 3

Kinlochbern Castle
Home of Laird MacDougal
Two weeks later...

The thick oak door held together by gleaming iron ties slammed shut, the sound reverberating throughout the great hall.

Barton MacDougal, the captain of the guard, strode to the dais where his laird was sitting, finishing his late afternoon meal.

Studying the man as he approached, Malcolm MacDougal dropped what remained of the roasted grouse leg and wiped his mouth and hands on a bit of linen. He might appreciate the warm, sticky, thick caress of blood—every once in a while, but the sensation of grease from roasted meat made his stomach turn.

"Barton," he said just after swallowing his last bite of grouse, "What have ye for me?"

Barton dipped his head a fraction in a clipped but acceptable sign of submission to his laird.

"Our *associate* within Gleneden was given explicit instruction tae watch and report, but tae continue their duties as usual," he replied, his cold eyes giving nothing away. "MacPherson is playin' right intae our hands, and once the noose 'round his neck is fitted perfectly, ye can draw it tight and hang him with it." The large man grinned a little at that, though his smile looked more like a grimace, one MacDougal had seen on that man's face more often of late. So what if Barton didn't quite appreciate his laird's plans; it didn't matter to MacDougal.

MacDougal sat back in his chair, his hands flat on the table before him. Relief nudged aside the wariness clinging to his every thought. At one time, not long ago, he believed his plan stalled, indefinitely, but then things turned around. It was a sign from God that he was in the right in seeking his vengeance against the hated MacPhersons, and all who allied with them over the years.

"Good, good," he drawled in clipped response to Barton, his tone lacking real pleasure. "And what of our deal with the Welshman?" The damn Welsh were unpredictable at best, but they were loyal, at least to those who offered them the most money, and this one had a skill set MacDougal had wanted in particular.

Barton nodded once, never one to waste a movement. "He is awaitin' yer summons, my laird."

"He damn well better be," MacDougal sneered, slapping the table with his palm, which made his whole hand tingle. "I willnae allow anyone tae ruin this for me...I have come too far, given too much."

Barton simply stared, and MacDougal suddenly hated how the man rarely showed a single sign of what he was thinking—except on those occasions when he was ordered to do something he considered untoward. It was disconcerting, though MacDougal knew that the man's utter lack of emotion was intimidating to the enemy. He was a tool, a weapon to use against that damn Dubhach MacPherson and all the blasted MacPhersons.

"If that is all, be gone. I have better things tae do than stare at yer ugly face any longer," MacDougal snapped, a shard of spittle flying from his mouth to land on the nearly empty trencher before him.

Again, without expression, Barton dipped his chin a fraction, then turned and strode from the room toward the kitchens, where MacDougal was sure he would snag a bit of leftover mutton pie. The man had many appetites; food, wine, women, and battle.

Grunting as he rose, pushing his chair back, MacDougal made his way from the large, empty, and echoing great hall to his private chambers. There, he took a piss, before walking to his armoire and opening it. The inside was mostly empty save for an altar of sorts, where nearly spent beeswax candles, a rosary, and a small silver urn were placed just so. The urn contained the ashes of his son, his beloved son, the son killed by the eldest son of Dairmaid MacPherson. The man he meant to ruin, just before burning everything he loved to the ground. Too bad the bastard died before MacDougal could finally find justice for his son. Then again, if a MacPherson still lived, there was still a chance at bloody recompense—he would make each of them pay.

Easing to the floor to kneel, he lit the candles and grasped the rosary, his heart aching as it did every day, every moment. His breath shuddering, he closed his eyes, the burn behind them a familiar sensation.

"Och, my boy..." he cried, "I mourn ye, I miss ye, the only true joy o' my life." He bent his head, his chin nearly touching his chest. A sob built in his throat and he allowed it release. "Ye will be avenged, my boy. I willnae rest 'til yer murderer knows the pain o' loss. Until he suffers as I have suffered. There will be an outcry like nae other, and all o' Kinloch Rannoch will hear the wails from Gleneden, and they will know that God has given us justice."

Just a bit longer, maybe another fortnight, and Malcolm MacDougal would watch as the MacPhersons were wiped from the earth, their history tainted with the blood of those they had destroyed on their way to wealth and power. There was no one alive who could stop him, he wouldn't allow it.

"Och, Bruce...if ye were here now, I would have ye smile. And we would both dance on the corpses o' those who have wronged us. I will see it done."

MacDougal rested there for long moments, his thoughts on his son, dead those these twenty-two years, and when he finally rose to his feet, his heart was lighter. His soul was burning hotter than it had been for months.

All was in place, his plots and schemes finally coming to head, and he could not wait to see the look on Thorn MacPherson's face when he thrust the point of his sword in the blackguard's heart.

Sighing, MacDougal quit his chamber, making his way to the courtyard were several of his men were sparring. He watched from the parapet over the open area of packed earth, which had turned to mud because of the relentless rain. But today, the sun was shining, the sky was blue, and nary a cloud in the sky. He took it as a sign that Bruce was smiling down at him, as eager and pleased about his father's plans as his father was.

Catching sight of Barton, MacDougal regarded the man as he sparred with his second-in-command, a man named Aubrey McGillivray. The McGillivray clan were allies with the MacDougals, though, they too, had seen much loss over the last several decades. With both of their clans dwindling in numbers, they'd shared their resources; men, harvests, and information. It was one of the McGillivray's that had overheard the cocky bastard MacPherson announce that he wouldn't marry until he'd found his long-lost betrothed. MacDougal had laughed at that, knowing full well the woman was long dead on a Welsh beach, her bones picked clean by scavengers.

He smiled at the thought, his cheeks aching from the unfamiliar stretching.

Shouts and grunts from below brought his attention back to the battle playing out before him. As expected, Barton was victorious; a vicious, deadly warrior who owed his life to MacDougal.

Barton looked up, spying MacDougal watching him. He inclined his head to his laird and MacDougal gave him a curt wave.

As a soft breeze slid over his cheek, MacDougal chose to believe that his darling Bruce were there with him. And he smiled again.

CHAPTER 4

The goddamn Scottish moors in a downpour
Maybe somewhere near Kinloch Rannoch, Scotland

Rose huddled beneath her cloak, cursing the sky for the near constant downpour over the last two days.

"Who the hell would live here voluntarily?" she groused, kicking a clump of mud out of her way as she hurried to a cluster of trees. Pulling her horse, Martle, behind her, she looped the steed's reins around a branch and patted him on his withers.

Martle nuzzled her hand and she smiled at him. "Not much farther, lad, then I will give you all the apples you can eat." At least she hoped it wasn't much farther.

It had been two weeks since that night in the Bearded Lady, where she met those two strangers.

William and Munro MacGuilliam. Two men who'd docked their cargo ship in the harbor and were looking for a little shore leave before they headed north along the west coast. She'd listened to them, asking questions, and the more they told her, the more she couldn't tear herself away. They were like bearded sirens with thick necks.

They'd told her what they knew about the crest on the locket, which wasn't much, but it was enough to stoke the fire that had been slowly dying to embers in her belly. The fire that had once driven her into recklessness before Ioan Rees, her "grandfather" put a leash around her neck. A leash made of purpose, a purpose she'd taken on as an oath she couldn't break.

But now...she was far from the home she knew, in a damn mud patch, trying to keep herself from dying of a chill before the sun rose again. If it ever did.

"What a godforsaken country," she mumbled to herself as she made her way under the thickest part of the branches, hoping they would keep off at least some of the rain. She shivered, sliding down the trunk to hug her knees, keeping the warmth as close to her body as possible.

Laying her cheek against her upright knees, she fought the urge to close her eyes.

Tired. So tired.

After that night of revelations with the MacGuilliam brothers, she'd gone straight upstairs to her room, packed a satchel, and then boarded their ship. She paid them for passage north, of course, but once the ship anchored in Loch Leven, she disembarked and didn't look back. She'd brought her horse with her, and once Martle had regained his land legs, they were off. It had taken several days to get a feel for the Scottish, but once she'd had a drink with a few of them, she realized just how much she liked them. In Wales, no one could hold a tankard to her iron stomach, but here...she'd nearly died during a drinking game with a Scotsman and his woman, both who'd come into the town she'd been passing through to celebrate their nuptials.

She bade them good tidings, and then wallowed on her own, in the stable where she'd taken refuge from, yet another, rain storm.

And now...she was out in the elements, hoping that the village of Kinloch Rannoch wasn't more than another day's travel. She didn't have much food left, and she'd never learned to hunt. Animals, anyway.

As Martle grazed in the rain, Rose let her mind wander. What would she do if she discovered the truth about what happened to her parents? What would happen if she stumbled upon a family she'd never thought to find? What would the Rees think of her leaving them without so much as a "fair sailing"? She knew the Rees would worry for her when she didn't return within a month, that they would, more than likely, come looking for her. But, before then, she hoped to learn more about her past. The past mired in missing memories and feelings of...not belonging.

Aye, the Rees had always welcomed her, making her one of their own, but she'd always know she wasn't truly a Rees. She remembered when Ioan Rees, the elder and former brenin, had found her on the beach, where she'd been wailing in confusion and fear. She couldn't remember what had happened to her, only that she was on a ship and then she wasn't. Ioan had promised to look after her, folding her into the family to be raised alongside his other grandchildren.

As her thoughts drifted into her past, her eyes began to droop.

So tired. When was the last time she'd slept through the night? When was the last time she could lie in bed, close her eyes, and not dream of black, suffocating, pounding water?

Something stirred her from her semi-slumber; the loss of sound. The rain had stopped.

Her eyes snapped opened, widening in her surprise at having fallen into slumber while sitting under a tree, in the pouring rain and brittle cold.

Shaking the drops of rain from her hair, she trembled as the water slid down the back of her neck and into the back of her shirt.

"Damn," she groused. "I'll never be dry again."

After the silence, there was a murmur and then a shout of laughter.

She held her breath, bending her ear to listen deeply.

Men. Maybe within several yards of where she was hunkered down.

Obviously, the loud pounding of the rain had drowned out the sounds of other people.

Swiftly gaining her feet, she continued to listen. Whoever they were, they weren't trying to hide their presence. They were loud, talking and shouting and practically drawing a target on their backs. A target in the shape of a red R. For Rose Red.

The corner of her mouth lifting into a sneer, she moved along the thick trunks of the trees, through the shadows, and right up to a line of trees just before a very small clearing.

In the clearing, there were five men, seated in a circle around a struggling fire. At least *they* were warm, at least *they* could get dry.

The men were wearing kilts, their swords strapped to their sides, and legs stretched out before them in a pose of ease.... These men had no idea how close they were to danger.

Leave them be, Rose, they are none of your concern. She wondered, though, who they were. Their kilts were all of the same pattern; varying blues, reds, black, gold and white. She'd heard of tartans before, but she'd never seen one with her own eyes. She knew that tartans designated to which laird or clan they swore allegiance.

Who did these men owe their allegiance to?

"...MacPherson has finally given up his quest for his missing bride," a man, second from the right, announced, and the other men mumbled their displeasure.

MacPherson? The name struck Rose like an arrow to the chest. The very same name the MacGuilliams had told her about; the clan with the symbol of the rose wrapped around the thorn as their crest. Tense, she continued to listen, her heart racing.

"Aye. There's rumor he is set tae marry his house wench."

"I've heard tales o' her, and how she'd been pinin' after MacPherson since she first grew tits." The man scowled, his lips curling. "She's a sight better than those whores who've been comin' in, claimin' tae be his long-lost betrothed. Those women are nae better than the tavern whore I bedded just last night."

"Wasnae that yer sister, Brandon?" the one closest to the fire quipped.

A man, apparently, Brandon, spat at him.

"Shut yer gob, Willy," Brandon sneered, leaning forward to give Willy a glare that looked more maniacal than menacing.

Rose bit back a chuckle. These men were no threat, but they could certainly give her information she'd been without since leaving the ship and finding her own way in a new and rugged territory.

Straightening, Rose placed a hand on her sword hilt, pasted a grin on her face, and stepped into the ring of firelight.

"Good evening, gentlemen," she drawled, and nearly fell into a heap of laughter at the looks of utter astonishment on their faces as they turned at the sound of her voice and stopped dead. "Can you kindly tell me where I can find Kinloch Rannoch." She sidled closer, her grin growing as the men blinked up at her, all of them caught up in the vision that was all Rose. "It seems I've lost my way."

CHAPTER 5

Thorn removed his boots, kicking them to the end of his bed where his two other pairs of boots were slumped. With his feet free of their confines, he wiggled his toes, thankful for the coolness of the stone floor.

He'd never liked wearing boots, had spent years of his life running amok in the woods outside Cylldon barefooted and carefree. And his foster father, the wise and patient Lord Lloyd Owains, had allowed it, not because he didn't care but because he understood that a man should be comfortable when facing down his fears. And Thorn had feared those woods...at least in the beginning.

When he'd first arrived at Cylldon as a lad of fourteen, preparing for his twenty years in another man's care, he'd gazed upon the dark woods surrounding the tall stone castle as if it were crawling with death. It had taken years before he braved the tangled veins and thick, low-hanging branches, but once he had...he'd tasted freedom for the first time.

For the last time.

A knock on his chamber doors pulled a sigh from his chest.

Rubbing the back of his neck, he knew he couldn't ignore her...

the woman he'd invited into his life. Permanently. The woman he had committed to marrying. The woman whose scent was strong enough for him to smell even through the door. Also, her knock was singular; two loud knocks and then a single soft tap. He'd gotten used to hearing it, but never on his own bedchamber door.

"Come," he called, beckoning his future wife into his private chambers, knowing full well what she was coming to ask him. Since offering for her, she'd become a whole new woman, brazen and possessive, and shrill.

Dear God, what have I gotten myself into?

He turned to watch as the thick oak door swung open and Briar glided through. Catching his gaze, she dipped her head, offering him a coy grin that, over the last several days, had begun to turn his stomach.

For the eighth or ninth time in the last week, he asked himself: *Was this all a mistake?*

And it didn't help that every time he pictured himself vowing to bind himself to Briar forever his stomach flipped, twisting.

God, if there were any way out of marrying at all, he would take it. But it was his duty as Laird MacPherson to wed, sire heirs, and provide a solid future for his people.

So, Briar MacPherson was his only choice, unless he wanted to marry one of the many women who'd lied to his face.

Nay.

"Why have you come, Briar?" he asked, not bothering to hide the annoyance in his voice.

Unbothered by his tone, she continued forward until she was within inches of him. Her scent, nigh overpowering, billowed up from where her breasts were heaving up and nearly falling out of her bodice. When he'd first seen her after having been gone so long, he could admit that his body responded to the sight of her large, plump breasts. But now....

"I have come to bid ye goodnight, husband," she drawled, raising her hand to run a finger along his naked chest. He was a large man, his muscles honed by hard work, sparring, and lack of idleness. He knew he was a fine specimen, a man every woman fawned over, but this one...her fawning felt forced.

It *all* felt forced.

What the hell has come over me? At one time, before his father's death and his subsequent rise to laird with all those damn duties, he'd looked forward to settling down with a good woman, siring a brood of strapping sons, and dying in old age with his family around him. But his father's death had rushed him headlong into something he couldn't fight against.

'Tis because I have no control over my own destiny.

Why had he ever thought to put off marrying by promising to only marry a woman who was probably long dead?

I am a fool beyond comparison.

"I can hear ye thinkin', lover," Briar muttered, her pout firmly in place. Since her rise to mistress-to-be of Gleneden, her façade of a submissive yet jealous spirit had slowly slipped away. In less than a week, Thorn had discovered the true Briar, one that used all her wiles to try and get him into her bed, or his. She'd purred and pouted, protesting that she'd waited long enough to have him for her own, but he'd rejected her advances, his flesh willing but his mind revolting. But it was too late to change his mind. What was done was done, and now he could only hope that things would work out in a way that would benefit them both. He'd have a wife to put a stop to the flood of faux fiancées, and she'd have his protection and...*him*.

"Why think when ye can lie with me...husband?" she said, pouting, her eyes dark with hunger.

"We are not married yet, woman," he snapped, and she narrowed her eyes, her pout turning from an attempt at sensual into a poorly disguised sneer.

"'Tis only a matter of a week, me love, and then I will be all ye will ever need," she said, her voice taking on a hard edge. "Remember, *husband*, ye asked *me*."

He stared down at her, into eyes blazing with arrogance and greed.

'Tis what you wanted.

Planting his hands on his hips, he waited for her to continue, though he already knew what she was going to say.

"Ye and I are tae be wed in a week's time...." Her finger returned to his chest, her fingernail flicking the flat head of his nipple. "And I cannae wait tae become *Lady MacPherson*."

"I do not suppose you can," he practically sneered, hating how his thoughts and emotions were in constant motion, never settling on one thing or another. It was exhausting.

"'Tis only a week, my love...." She dropped her hand, reaching down to cup his bollocks, and squeezing.

He stiffened and she grinned, believing his response was one of arousal. It wasn't. It was vexation. Thorn was a healthy man with a healthy appetite for sex, and aye, Briar was a beautiful, sensual woman. He would bed her, often, but on his terms.

Take, appease her, slake your own lusts.... What man would deny himself such a lush offering? Again, his thoughts and emotions wavered, and he snagged the most immediate emotion, one that *needed.*

He allowed the need for physical pleasure to override all else.

"You wish for pleasure, my dear?" He asked, his arms snaking out to wrap around her waist. She gasped and then purred, leaning into his embrace. Her breasts pressing against the hardness of his chest. Immediately, his manhood stiffened, his body responding though his mind wasn't engaged.

As an animal would. He forced down the indignation that notion ignited. He was no better than an animal anyway, seeking his pleasure despite all that felt wrong about it.

Father would be ashamed of me.

Growling—angry at himself—he leaned down to take her lips, burning with a new need to numb all higher reasoning, but a pounding on the door made him jerk to a stop.

Briar hissed at the interruption, but Thorn dropped his arms, taking a step away from her, and then called, "Come," for the second time in fifteen minutes.

The door opened quickly, and Garrick stepped inside the room, his knowing gaze flicking from Thorn to Briar and back.

"What is the meanin' o' this interruption?" Briar snarled, her practiced comeliness gone in a blink.

Garrick didn't apologize, not that he ever would, and his eyes remained hooded and yet all-seeing.

"There is a...commotion," he answered—to Thorn. The man knew his loyalties were to his laird, and not to Briar. Not yet anyway.

Stepping around Briar, Thorn intoned, "Commotion? What do you mean? 'Tis late, Garrick, I care not if the men are making fools of themselves."

Garrick's expression didn't change. "Five o' the men on patrol were attacked, my lord—"

That snapped Thorn from his already fleeting thoughts of returning to what he'd been doing before Garrick arrived. "Attacked? By who?" he growled, wrath snaking through his spine.

"Most likely MacDougal men, but I cannae know for sure. I think it best ye speak with them," Garrick remarked, moving aside to allow Thorn to stride past him and through the door.

Behind Thorn, Briar followed, her belligerent gaze poking holes into his back.

They made it down the stairs and to the door to the great hall quickly, Thorn's heart pounding, his chest heaving, as his anger grew.

Who would dare attack his men on his land? Whoever they were, they would know the brutal and merciless hand of justice.

Storming through the door, his mouth opening to command answers, but the breath leaving his body stole all the words he meant to speak.

There, standing in the midst of bruised and bloody men, was a woman more stunning than he had ever seen in his lifetime.

Long red hair was confined to a thick braid that hung over her shoulder to just under her plump, pale breasts. The shirt she was wearing was open enough to only give him a glimpse of what was hidden beneath, but it was enough, because as soaked as she was from the evening's rain, he could see the outline of her nipples through the thin fabric. As if by instinct, the need to suck those same nipples into his mouth made his tongue flick against his teeth.

Damn.

Forcing down the urge to suckle her, he continued his perusal of her. Her face was the color of toasted cream, and her eyes were a brown that brought to mind the decadent desserts he'd favored.

And those eyes...they were pinned to him, unblinking and filled with curiosity. She was appraising him openly, unabashedly, taking in his naked chest, his legs encased in leather breeches, and then landing on his manhood. It twitched at the attention, not that he blamed it; he too was enjoying this woman's heated gaze far more than he should.

Who is she?

"Who are ye?" Briar demanded from beside him, her voice shrill.

Blinking, Thorn realized what a fool he must look like, barging into the great hall only to stop dead and stare at the newcomer.

The woman shrugged, her braid sliding off her shoulder to swing behind her. As long as it was, he had no doubt the very tip of it would brush against her arse. And she was wearing black leather breeches, her long legs practically naked—the leather being as tight as it was. He could make out the bones in her knees, for Christ sake!

One of the men, Brandon, stepped forward, wiping at a bit of dried blood on his lips.

"Tell me what happened, Brandon—and be quick about it. It looks like you lot have had a night of it."

"We were preparin' tae head out on the last patrol o' the night, when we heard a woman, screamin'. O' course we went tae see what was the matter, and we came upon this lass—eight men 'round her, threatenin' tae kill her, but nae a'fore they used her."

Shocked, Thorn's gaze snapped to the woman, and something made him pause.

She didn't look like someone who'd just been saved from the clutches of eight rapists. The woman was standing straight, her shoulders back, her head tipped to the side, watching him silently. There wasn't a single mark on her either, at least none that he could see.

"And you saved her?" Thorn asked, dragging his attention back to Brandon.

His face bloomed red. "Aye," he answered, his head nodding vigorously. Comically. As though he didn't know what to do with it.

"And they were not MacDougal's men?" The men all shook their heads.

"And you, who are you?" he finally asked her, the woman who had stolen his breath.

She took a step forward, and that was when he noticed a sword, strapped to her side, and her hand gripping the handle with white knuckles.

So, she was both armed and not as unaffected as she let on.

"Who are *you*?" she asked, a blazing red eyebrow arching upward.

Briar hissed. "How dare ye speak tae our laird in such a manner—"

Thorn lifted a hand to silence her, and she bit back whatever else she was about to spew.

"'Tis fine. I understand how...frightened and uncertain she must be. After all, she was nearly violated. 'Tis good you men were there to save her...."

His gaze scouring the woman's expression, he noticed something flashing over her face—but it was gone in an instant.

"I am Dubhach MacPherson, Laird of Gleneden, and this is my home," he answered, spreading his arms wide. Her eyes missed nothing, trailing over the bulges of muscles in his arms, over his shoulders, and finally back to his face. She smirked, her lush lips quirking at the sides.

His body tightened at the sight.

What is it about this woman? She was a complete stranger, a puzzle, and she hadn't answered the damn question.

"Now, tell me who you are, and how you came to be on my land in the dead of night where you could be set upon by blackguards?"

"You may call me Red," she answered, her voice a husky and supple sound that immediately caressed his manhood. "And I must...*thank* your men for rescuing me." She raised her hands to just under her chin, and she batted her eyelashes. "Oh, I cannot imagine what would have happened if these strapping men had not come to save me."

The men—all five of them—blushed, ducking their heads as if to hide their expressions.

What was really going on? If she'd been attacked, the men wouldn't be the only ones with bloody lips and the tell-tale signs of bruising on their cheeks and eyes.

Crossing his arms over his chest, he commanded, "You five, rouse Marcus, have him tend your wounds." The men almost collided with one another in their rush to leave.

A strangled snort sounded from Garrick, who'd been watching the scene with wide eyes. He too knew something was amiss.

And I will uncover the truth.

CHAPTER 6

"Red, was it? Will you please follow me?" He raised an arm, pointing to the door leading to the corridor, that led to his personal study. It was a large room, lined with thick tapestries, hunting trophies, and portraits of his ancestors. It had belonged to his father, not more than four years ago, but in that time, he hadn't changed anything, hadn't put his own touch on the room.

Because it would always be his father's, even though he was the laird now. It still felt wrong to touch something that had belonged to a man he'd admired and adored, a man whose passing had torn the heart out of every single MacPherson.

I can only hope to be a quarter the leader my father was.

As Thorn walked, he didn't need to look behind him to know that the woman was following him; he could feel her, like a fire burning into him with every step.

Pushing through the study door, he strode to the desk then turned to watch as she entered behind him. When she did, he noticed—unhappily—that his betrothed had followed him as well. Before he could tell her to leave, she closed the door behind her, the haughty lift of her chin telling him that she believed it was her place to follow him, and no doubt shutting the door in Garrick's face.

Knowing Garrick, the man would gladly leave them to their business. Still it bothered him that the woman, who was not yet his wife, had acted with such authority.

Red—if that was her name at all—glided across the floor, her movements agile, smooth, almost elegant, and she plopped herself down in the chair.

Behind the desk.

Thorn knew he should feel anger at her obvious disregard for his dominion, but he couldn't. There was a tightness in his chest when he looked at her, a spark of light, a flickering of interest.

It was unlike anything he'd felt before, and he wanted to know more. To feel more of *this*—whatever it was.

Briar stalked toward Red, her face hard and her cheeks pink with displeasure. She stopped just in front of Red who was leaning back in the chair, staring at Thorn, her gaze never leaving his face. Never in his life had he been the subject of such intense study before, and he couldn't say he didn't like it.

Sneering down at Red, Briar huffed. "Ye had better start explainin' whatever it is that really happened. And what sort of woman wears men's breeches? 'Tis unseemly!" she snapped.

"Briar," Thorn barked, his patience with the woman growing thinner by the moment. "I believe it is late and you should be retiring for the evening."

She opened her mouth to protest, but he pierced her with a look that told her to keep her mouth shut and do what she was told.

Her expression softening in a flash, she sauntered up to Thorn, throwing her arms around his neck, and planting a kiss on his lips. He wasn't a fool, he knew she was claiming him in front of the newcomer. And it irked him more than it should.

"I will be waitin' for ye, husband," she purred as she pulled away to throw one last glare over her shoulder at Red, before hurrying from the room.

The door slammed behind her, the sound echoing throughout the chamber.

And finally, they were alone. Thorn regarded the woman behind his desk silently, watching as the flickering fire in the hearth cast brightness and shadow over her face. And what a stunning face it was. Her cheekbones were high but finely made, and her dark eyes were the shape of almonds, rimmed with dark red lashes that fanned whenever she blinked. Which wasn't often.

She was unsettling.

He drew himself to his full height, noticing that, once again, her gaze followed his movements, seeming to devour him, bite by bite.

"Now," he began, leaning down to plant his hands on the top of his desk. "Why don't you tell me what really happened?"

Her eyes danced in response, and she pursed her lips, drawing the plumper bottom lip into her mouth where she bit it. He nearly groaned, the need to do the same to her lips rising quickly and hotly.

"I do not know what you mean, my lord. I was rescued from a most terrible fate," she answered, her face lighting up with barely hidden mirth.

He snorted. "Why do I not believe that?"

She shrugged. "How am I to know, I am not you."

He was both frustrated and entertained by the wench, and that was new to him. Usually, when dealing with impertinent women, he'd order them to leave, or put their mouths to better use elsewhere. At that thought, an image of her tempting mouth wrapped around his girth made his manhood press against his breeches.

Damn!

"You mean to continue deceiving me, woman? You carry a sword, you wear men's breeches, and you do not speak as a Scottish lass...." If he hadn't been so shaken by the sight of her, he would have immediately recognized her accent as Welsh. It was an accent he'd heard for most of his life, having spent his majority with the Owains.

She gave a lopsided grin. "Neither do you, my lord," she remarked, the emphasis on *my lord.*

"What is a Welshwoman doing in Kinloch Rannoch—" It hit him then. *She is here to play me false, to claim that she is my long-lost betrothed. She is just like the others.*

Immediately, his interest in her dimmed. She was just another opportunist, looking to scheme her way into his bed, and into his clan.

"You can stop with the pretense, wench," he said, his voice hard. "If you had not noticed, I am already promised to wed. Your scheme has come a week too late."

As with the other women he'd denied, he expected her to jump up, affronted, then fall to her knees, beginning him to give her a chance to prove herself.

But she didn't do that. She remained where she was, in his chair, her hands on her lap, her gaze on his face.

"You are right," she confessed. "I *have* schemed."

His triumph at her confession was paltry, not nearly as fulfilling as he'd wanted.

Pushing away from his desk, he crossed his arms. Again, noticing her noticing him.

"You admit it, then, your wish to seduce me into your bed, then beg me to pledge my troth?" Why was he pushing this? Why was his blood thickening in his veins, and why was he enjoying the feeling of the strange and heady tension growing between them?

"Seduce you?" She snorted. "If I meant to do that, I would have been bent over this desk the moment we walked through the door—your betrothed could have watched."

His heart thudding, he nearly shook his head to clear out the cobwebs, for certain, he didn't just hear what he thought he heard.

"Who are you?" he asked, his voice a deep whispered awe.

She grinned at him, her straight white teeth flashing, making her beauty all the more brilliant. All the more breathtaking.

"I am Rose Rees," she answered, her tone tinkling with unspent laughter.

"Rees?" He knew that name. One didn't live in Wales without hearing that name whispered in the darkened corners of taverns, or in well-lit meetings with nobles frustrated by their missing goods. "You are a pirate, then?" he sneered.

She giggled—*giggled*—before standing and extending her hand in a gesture probably meant to appease.

He glared down at it.

"You want to know the truth, my lord," she offered, coming around the desk to stand before him, her head tipped up to meet his gaze with her unrepentant and fearless eyes.

Oh, this should be interesting, indeed.

CHAPTER 7

Rose fought the urge to reach out and pet the large, gorgeous man before her. Damn, but he was the perfect mix of muscles, lithe grace, and masculine beauty. He looked like one of the marble statues her cousin Lucian had brought back after a smuggling run to Athens.

Without wavering, Rose allowed the man to continue his perusal of her person. It wasn't as though she hadn't been doing the same to him since he stormed into the great hall, his heaving chest bare, and his glorious face a hard mask of anger.

Ooo, she liked 'em angry, especially in bed. The angrier the sex, the more passionate, the more pleasurable.

She nearly shuddered at the thought of bedding the man before her.

I will...but not yet. Not until I get what I need from him. Then, she could climb him like a mast and furl his sails.

Then again...her memory of the pouty-faced harridan who'd accompanied her lord made Rose inwardly cringe. Nay. Despite what she'd said earlier about his betrothed watching, she wasn't one to dally with another woman's goods. She'd seen what sort of chaos that could create; her grandfather Ioan having dallied with many a married woman after his own wife ran away from him, and then having to fend off those cuckolded husbands at the point of his sword.

Sighing, Rose dropped her smile, knowing that trying to entice the man would only cause problems she didn't want to deal with on top of everything else.

"Dubhach...what does it mean?" she asked, trying to fill the heavy air with words of little meaning.

"Thorny." His answer was clipped, as though he didn't want to discuss it.

"Hell you say?" she said, gaping at him. "Is that a jest?"

He shook his head, a slight smile on his face. "Nay, 'tis a theme. I am Thorn, named in honor of the family crest."

The family crest with the rose that wound around the thorn. Damn. The symbolism was heavy with the MacPhersons, and the fact that her name was Rose absolutely did not make her heart stutter.

Must find out about this locket. That was her prime objective. That, and getting something to eat. She hadn't had meat in days, and her belly was screaming for a shot of whiskey.

"Can I trouble you for a bite to eat...my lord, and perhaps some dry clothes?" she asked, her tone softer, docile, a tone her cousins would gawp at in horror.

The man, *Dubhach*, narrowed his eyes at her, scouring her expression for signs of something. Deception perhaps. She'd already told him she'd tell him all about her scheme, and it certainly wasn't whatever scheme he thought she was running. Who played at being someone's betrothed? It seemed like inviting a whole ocean of agony wedded to a lifetime of rotting boredom.

He sighed, his broad shoulders lifting and then falling, as if he were adjusting an invisible weight, then he turned and strode to the door. His long legs were thick with muscles that his leather breeches caressed as she would have...if he weren't betrothed.

She was a woman of *some* honor, after all.

Opening the door, he murmured to someone on the other side, before closing the door firmly and striding back toward her. She remained where she was by his imposing desk, her arms crossed over her chest. Unthinkingly, she reached up to finger the locket that was usually there, only to find it gone. Immediately she remembered that she'd removed it, secreting it in a hidden pocket at the back of her breeches. She was traveling into a land she didn't know, and so she didn't trust that anyone who saw it would act favorably toward her.

According to the MacGuilliam brothers, the crest belonged to a powerful and old Scottish clan, but Rose didn't know what that meant. Would that make her enemies with whoever she encountered, simply because she wore a MacPherson crest around her neck? Nay, it was safer to hide it. At least until she knew more.

So, find out more, her thoughts prodded her.

The laird of the castle pointed to a set of chairs beside the hearth. "Let us sit, converse, while we wait for Garrick to return."

"And if you cannot find fit to call me Dubhach, you may call me *my laird*, MacPherson, or Thorn."

Thorn. And Rose. She wanted to throw back her head and laugh at that.

"Thorn it is, then," she replied, grinning at him.

Following his lead, Rose walked to the chairs and took the one facing the door. One could never be too careful, especially when surrounded by threat on all sides.

Thorn eased himself into the other chair, crossing his ankle over his knee. His gaze bore into her, and she let him look. She wasn't shy, and she knew he would only ever see what she wanted him to see. She hadn't spent years perfecting her unaffected expression for it to fail now.

Leaning back, she waited for him to speak, to ask the questions she knew were burning a hole in his head.

Finally, he inquired, "What really happened with those men?"

"I met them, not far from here, and asked them to help me find my way to Kinloch Rannoch," she answered simply.

He arched a black brow, his dark whiskey-colored eyes flickering with interest.

"No attack? No near rape?"

She shook her head, "Aye and nay."

His brows furrowed. "'Tis late and I find myself weary of this encounter; can you not speak plainly?"

Suddenly, something akin to guilt pricked at her. She'd felt it before, just not often.

"I came upon your men as they chattered around their fire like a cackling of hens. I asked them to show me the way to Kinloch Rannoch, and they seemed unwilling to provide me with the help I needed. So...I offered them a wager."

"Wager for what?"

She dipped her face to hide the flush of pleasure that rose into her cheeks at the memory.

"I wagered that they couldn't best me, and if, by some chance they could, I would give them my horse."

His beautiful lips cocked up on the side.

"And if you won?"

She shrugged. "They would escort me to where I needed to go, and I would swear to never tell a soul that they had their bollocks removed by a mere woman."

Thorn threw his head back and laughed, the taut ropes of his neck flexing most deliciously. She groaned, the urge to lick him there nearly toppling her from her chair.

"From the looks of them, they lost the wager...and your *scheme* was the lie about them rescuing you from blackguards."

She chuckled. "Aye."

"And the rest of it? Why were you looking for Kinloch Rannoch?"

"Here is the whole of it, then," she began, and he clasped his fingers in his lap as a child would before listening to a tall tale. "I am looking for information, and someone told me I could find it here. I have been traveling for weeks, and when I came upon your men speaking the name MacPherson, I knew I had finally come to the right place."

"What information?" his expression was one of wary intrigue. "What do you want with me?"

Her lips quirked, her gaze immediately dropping to where his manhood was nestled between his legs. He shifted in his seat and she grinned.

"I have something, a locket, and on it is the impression of a rose, it's stem twined around a thorn."

He nodded. "The crest of the MacPherson clan."

"'Tis what I was told," she admitted.

"And where is this locket?" he asked.

"I have it, hidden."

"And you are wondering what, exactly?"

"I want to know about the man who gave it to me," she answered, her heart slowly rising into her throat. This was it...she was so close to knowing, even just a sliver, of what had eluded her for so long.

He arched an eyebrow, his face unreadable. "And who gave it to you?"

She took a deep breath then uttered, "My father."

He seemed taken aback by that, his chin lifting as he leaned back. "How is it that you do not know of your father but you know it was your father who gave it to you?"

Rose expected these questions, and so she answered quickly, "I do not remember much of anything about him, save that the locket was a gift from him. His name was Angus. And he died in a shipwreck."

He grunted, his eyes flying wide even as his face lost all color.

She held her breath, wondering what just happened.

"Angus, you say?" he inquired, his voice deadly flat.

She nodded once.

"Angus...surname?" he continued.

She pondered that question for a moment. Rose never could remember what her last name had been, and she'd spent the majority of her life calling herself Rees. "I assume he was a MacPherson because the locket he gave me has the MacPherson crest on it."

He leaned forward, his body tense, like a mooring chain in a storm.

"And you said your name was *Rose*?" This time, his voice was tight, deep, sending a tremor of warning up her spine. She stiffened, her hand itching to curl around her sword.

"Aye, I am Rose. 'Tis the name I remember him calling me," she admitted warily.

Silence followed her words, and it seemed as though the world was holding its breath, waiting, watching, anticipating.

Rose didn't know what Thorn would ask next, his expression hard as granite, his large body humming with leashed emotions. But what he *did* ask made Rose blink at him in uncharacteristic shock.

"Would you mind removing your breeches?"

Stunned, she waited to see if he would grin and then laugh off his words as a jest.

He did not. He simply stared at her, the question hanging in the air between them.

"What?" she finally croaked. She swallowed the lump of uncertainty and feigned nonchalance. "You want me to remove my breeches?"

He planted his elbows on his thighs and steepled his fingers. "Aye."

She offered him a lopsided grin, one she didn't actually feel. "And what will your *betrothed* think of that?"

He scowled, waving off her concern. "I only wish to see the flesh of your left buttock," he remarked as though it was something he asked of women every day.

"My left buttock? Why? What are you hoping to see?" Lord, but her curiosity would lead her into trouble—again. She wasn't a shy woman, she had no issue with striding around her own chambers naked, no matter who was in the room with her. But this...it was new.

"I will tell you once I have examined your left buttock," he pressed, and she grunted in response.

"Well then," she growled. "If you wish to see my left arse cheek, then you will get the whole show, my lord."

Rising to her feet, she quickly loosened the breeches by undoing the leather thongs holding them together in the front. Turning, she slipped her thumbs under the waistband, looking over her shoulder at Thorn with a blatant glare, then pushed the breeches down over her arse until her waistband caught on her thighs. She lifted the bottom of her sopping wet shirt to give him a better view.

Behind her, Thorn was quiet, and she wondered what he thought of her arse. She knew it was plump, two orbs of fleshy lushness that many a bedmate had nibbled and complimented. But...she knew that her *assets* weren't what Thorn was looking for. Sadly.

Craning her neck backward, Rose tried to see what Thorn was seeing. What was he looking for that could only be found on her arse?

Finally, the silence was broken by the hiss of an indrawn breath.

"'Tis you," Thorn murmured and she dropped her shirt and spun on her heel, coming face to face with a man who looked like he'd just seen a ghost.

Her heart thundering, her hands trembling, she couldn't fathom the dread pooling in her belly.

"Who do you think I am?" she asked, hating how weak her voice sounded.

He drew in a breath, his chest shuddering, his voice was deep, reaching into her chest.

"You are Rosette MacDeargh, the only daughter of Angus MacDeargh, clan chief and laird of Dearghrose Castle. You are goddaughter to my father, Dairmaid MacPherson, and...." He sucked in a shaky breath, his massive body shuddering. "...my true betrothed."

Weighing a million tons, the revelations made her fall back, landing against the side of the desk. She caught herself before she landed on her naked arse on the floor.

"Nay, 'tisn't possible," she murmured, unaware that Thorn had come to stand before her. His large hands reached out, cupping her face and tipping her chin up, forcing her to meet his awestruck gaze. Her breath caught.

"I never thought to find you," he whispered, his black eyes wide, an edge of wariness within. Then, a tapestry of determination and stone cold resolve wove itself together over his features, and his next words made the fibers holding Rose together fray at the edges. "And I never mean to lose you again."

CHAPTER 8

Rose struggled to get her waistband up over the curves of her generous arse, an arse where the birthmark in the shape of a rose petal rested on the fleshy part of her left buttock.

"You are mistaken," she ground out before slapping at his hands, which were still cupping her smooth, flawless face. He held fast, unwilling to let her go, to let her slip away again. She narrowed her eyes at him, the deep decadent brown darkening until it was nearly black.

God, she was a fiery one.

"Even if I am this Rosette MacDeargh, I am *not* your betrothed," she growled, finally pulling away. He dropped his hands, his fingers fisting at his sides to keep from reaching for her again.

This will take time. But it had already been twenty-six years since their fathers had signed the contract that bound their children together. At the time, Thorn had been a strapping lad of nine, and his wife-to-be was no more than an infant. He'd known, then, what his duty was, and he fully intended to follow through with the marriage, once they were both of age. But then...the business with MacDougal began, his threats against the MacPhersons turning ugly. Rosette's father feared for her life, and so he decided to take her to Wales, to Cylldon, to foster with the Owains as well. But on the journey south to Cylldon, their ship was lost, never making it to port in Bangor. When he'd heard that his betrothed, the sweet and fiery Little Rose, was last seen unconscious on a beach somewhere in Wales, he'd feared for her life in his own way. They hadn't known one another all that well, but he still worried for her, and he grieved for his father who had lost his dear friend.

After the one surviving sailor had returned to Kinloch Rannoch, telling his father that he had pulled a living, breathing Rosette from the sea, his father swore that there was still a chance that Rose was alive and well somewhere in Wales. Thorn had assumed his father was being a hopeful fool, a man whose grief had stolen a bit of his sense. But Thorn couldn't argue with his father, and he went about his life, living and learning beside his foster brothers and sisters, all the while wondering what did happen to Little Rose.

And now he knew.

She'd grown into a devastatingly beautiful woman, with hair of fire, eyes of guilty pleasure, and a body he couldn't wait to feel beneath him. And...from the conversation he'd had with her so far, her wit was razor sharp, her intelligence high.

"Are you not going to say something?" she snapped, crossing her arms over her chest which only served to push her breasts up, revealing more of the creamy globes to his hungry gaze.

She saw him looking, pursing her lips in a show of an emotion he had not seen thus far: annoyance.

For the first time that evening, he grinned, flashing his teeth at the woman before him. He knew what his smile looked like and how it affected the gentler sex. It would be no different for Rose, who'd already ogled him openly since setting eyes on him.

But, not for the first time and probably not for the last, she didn't do what he expected.

She lifted both eyebrows and cursed. "Well, if all you are going to do is grin at me in silence, I am going to get the hell out of here." She flung her arm into the air angrily and dismissively, and turned to walk away.

Do not let her go!

Reaching out, Thorn snagged her wrist and, in a flash, she swung around, her fist connecting with his belly. If he wasn't a fit and muscular man, her blow would have him doubled over. As it was, she'd landed a hit that would leave a bruise, and he knew damn well her fist would hurt like the devil.

Rose grunted, recoiling to shake her hand as if to rid herself of the pain. Her expression was hard, her cheeks flushed with an utterly becoming rage. She was glorious when she was wrathful, and he would enjoy riling her up...in the bedroom.

With that in mind, he grinned again, hoping this smile would dispel some of her displeasure.

"Come now, Rose, there is much to discuss," he entreated, making sure to keep his voice soft and even. They hadn't been reunited long, but he could already surmise that once Rose was wary, it would be difficult to sway her. His gaze immediately dropped to the sword at her hip. It looked perfectly at home where it was, which begged the question...what had she experienced in her life that had turned her into a sword-wielding, breeches-wearing, vision of danger and sensuality?

You will never know if you cannot get her to stay.

"Garrick has yet to arrive with your food or change of clothes," he reminded her. "The least I can do is feed you and get you dry, and you can ask me the questions I know are swirling in your head."

Rose cocked her head, her narrowed eyes scouring his face. He knew what she was searching for; deception and ill-intent. She'd find neither of those things. She was his betrothed, he owed her his honesty.

Finally, Rose nodded, and just as she did, a knock sounded at the door. He had little time to appreciate her acquiescence, as tremulous as it was.

"Come!" he called, knowing Garrick had arrived with Rose's food. The door opened and Garrick entered carrying a tray holding a slab of beef, a wedge of bread, and a mug of ale.

Garrick made eye contact, a question burning in his eyes. Thorn offered him an expression that said *I will tell you all later...*

"Have Marbeth leave the clothes in a guest chamber," Thorn ordered, knowing Marbeth would be beyond curious to know about the woman who'd shown up out of nowhere and was staying the night.

If I can get Rose to stay the night, that is.

Without a word, Garrick placed the tray on Thorn's desk, and Rose lifted her face, sniffing the air, before taking the chair behind the desk once more.

Rose tore into the bread, dipping a piece of it into the gravy from the beef. She bit into her meal with zeal and passion, and he couldn't tear his eyes away from what she was doing with her mouth. Thorn didn't know when Garrick had left but he didn't care, his focus was trained on the woman who had just licked her plump lips, her pink tongue doing dangerous things to his manhood.

Swallowing, Thorn grabbed a chair from beside the hearth and carried it, setting it beside Rose's so they were both seated behind his desk. He watched her eat, wondering when she'd eaten last, as she didn't stop eating until there were only bread crumbs remaining.

Downing the last of her ale, she slammed the mug onto the desk and let out a belch that would put any of his men to shame.

He cringed, shocked at his own lack of reaction to her lack of feminine decorum.

Her gaze snapped to his, her flame-red brow curling up. One side of her mouth cocked upward in a smirk that did awful, terrible, delicious things to his body.

"Not the delicate lady you were hoping for?" she drawled, her smirk growing.

She thought her show of ribald behavior would turn him away?

Not bloody likely.

Ignoring her self-deprecating comment, he leaned back in his chair and clasped his hands in his lap, a countenance of calm and patience.

"You have questions," he prompted, just before she flicked her tongue out to lick the beef juices from her fingers. One. At. A. Time. His bollocks drew up tight, his shaft swelling. Damn. He'd never been so aroused by someone eating.

Get a hold of yourself, Thorn! The last thing he needed was to allow his body to steer the rest of the evening, not when there was so much to say, to ask.

"I do have questions," she replied. "First one is what is it that you saw on my arse that made you so bloody convinced that I am your betrothed?"

He bit back a laugh. "How do you not know what is on your own arse?" What a strange conversation he was diving headlong into. And he was thoroughly enjoying himself already.

She snorted. "I am not an owl, I cannot turn my head so far as to see what is on my own arse cheek."

He did laugh then, a chest rattling chuckle that shook something from his shoulders. A weight. One of a million.

"A mirror, then," he quipped.

Incredulous, her mouth and eyes wide, she gasped. "What sort of person admires their own arse in a mirror?" She huffed, crossing her arms and throwing him a look that only made his face break into a smile.

"A lover, then? Has no one told you about the mark shaped like a rose petal on your left buttock?"

A bark of laughter escaped. "I can promise you they were too busy admiring the shape of my arse rather than the shape of a flaw on my skin."

A spark of anger lit him from the inside. "It is not a flaw," he ground out.

"Then what would you call it?" she asked.

He leaned forward, dropping his hands between his thighs, and pinned her with his gaze.

"The mark that allowed me to welcome you home, where you belong, Rose."

CHAPTER 9

Rose couldn't peel her eyes away from the intensity of Thorn's gaze.

"You are mad," she murmured, shaking her head in disbelief.

"Not mad. I just cannot believe that, after all this time, you are here, you are alive—where have you been all this time?" There was an awe in his voice.

"I have been in Wales, with the Rees," she answered simply, being careful to keep the more...infamous information to herself.

His expression took on an edge, one that made her tense.

"How did that happen?" he asked. "You survived a shipwreck...." He was prodding her, and she didn't like it. But there was a sense of need that made her want to tell him something.

"I somehow made it ashore and was found by the man who would become my grandfather, Ioan Rees."

"One of the sailors rescued you, bringing you to shore. But, he lost consciousness shortly thereafter and once he came to again, you were gone."

That was new information. Nay, she'd always known the chances of a small child swimming to shore on her own were nigh impossible, but she had never considered that someone had rescued her.

"And this rescuer, he told you about the shipwreck?" she asked, cautiously.

"Aye. He came home several weeks later and told my father. My father sent word to me in Wales."

Surprised, she asked, "Why were you in Wales?"

"That is a story for another time, Little Rose."

She scrunched up her nose at the nickname he'd given her, a nickname that didn't bother her as much as it should. She didn't know him, he didn't know her, so the familiarity was strange.

"If you were in Wales, why did you not look for me? You knew I was last seen on the beach, could you not have searched for me?"

Rose watched him swallow, then lick his lips. "I was young. My life consisted of lessons during the mornings, adventure in the afternoons, and evenings with my foster father."

Foster father? She opened her mouth to ask about him, but she realized that was part of whatever it was he did not want to speak about just then. She inwardly shrugged. She didn't really care to learn Thorn's history, only where it pertained to her history. To her family.

"You have questions for me, then?" she offered, wanting to fill the growing tension in the air with something else for it to bang against.

Thorn didn't move, and Rose wondered if he was breathing. Examining his naked chest for signs of respirations, she inwardly groaned at all the tanned muscle on display.

Focus! He is betrothed to be married, and since you are not his betrothed you cannot have what you want.

"Someone found you on the beach...."

"Aye," she answered. Drawing her shoulders back, she continued, "Ioan Rees found me, raised me, bringing me into the fold of the Rees family."

"Pirates," he interjected.

"Smugglers," she corrected. "We never attack ships or people, we offer our logistics services to people in need of them. We move goods without ever laying a hand on innocent people."

She might be a slightly immoral hellion but she'd never hurt anyone who didn't deserve it. The Rees considered themselves noble villains, angels with crooked halos, scoundrels with hearts of gold.

"And you remember nothing of the shipwreck?"

She shook her head. "I remember most of what happened just before. It was calm and then it wasn't, and the sea battered the ship, and my father...." Her throat closed up against the words. At night, in the dark and silence, the dreams would come. The memories that wove with the nightmare, the nightmare that stole her slumber, drove her to numb her fear in whiskey and mindless sex with strangers.... She'd lost her innocence at thirteen to a man more than twice her age. He'd been gentle and yet forceful, taking his pleasure. It had been unlike anything she'd expected; there'd been pain and shame and some enjoyment, but it was what she realized afterward that had made her return for that same encounter over and over again, with different men in different ports for thirteen years. For a short time during the experience, she hadn't felt *misplaced*, like she didn't belong.

That need for belonging had festered within her for as long as she could remember. Aye, she'd been adopted into the Rees, but she knew she wasn't one. She knew she had a family elsewhere, that she was missing a part of herself, and that the family she didn't know about was maybe missing her, too.

But she could tell no one, they would think her weak, vulnerable, unworthy of their trust on matters as vital as gathering information for the family. Aye, Saban, her eldest cousin, would understand, he knew what it was like to live with so much responsibility on his shoulders, but Rose didn't want to add to that, to become a burden when she only ever wanted to be...found.

Lost. So lost in thought....

Reaching out, Thorn placed his large hand over hers, grasping it gently.

"Do you...remember me?" Did *he* remember *her*? From the looks of him, he couldn't be more than thirty-five, and at her age of six and twenty, she couldn't have been much older than a mewling babe when they were betrothed to one another. Did a lad remember the little girl he was promised to marry? And if he did, what did he remember about her?

A slowly growing desire to know all the answers to all the questions bloomed in her mind.

After all these years of feeling adrift in her own life, could it be as simple as speaking with the man before her?

Blinking the haze from her eyes, Rose noticed the change in him, how his shoulders tensed, his eyes becoming hooded, as though he were hiding his vulnerable parts from her.

"Do you remember me, Rose? We were betrothed just after you were born, but we had four years together after that. You might remember some of that," he coaxed, this time his voice carrying a note of restraint. Rose could sense he was holding himself back, probably containing his urge to shake the truth from her. But she didn't know all the truths—she was seeking her own.

Did it really matter to him that much, that she remember him? *Did* she remember him?

If she were really the Rosette MacDeargh he thought she was, wouldn't she have remembered him? At least by name? Rose bit the inside of her cheek, using the sharp pain to focus her mind.

She tried to imagine what Thorn might look like as a young lad, dark-haired, perhaps gangly and pale, but still with those striking jet-colored eyes.

Nothing.

Shifting in her seat, she sighed. "Nay. Sorry, I cannot remember you," she admitted.

Unexpectedly, Thorn didn't look all that disappointed, or even surprised.

"You were young, 'tis understandable that you wouldn't remember me," he admitted. His upper lip curled up just slightly, and Rose was fascinated by the movement. He had such lovely lips for a man. 'Twas almost a crime that God had given him such perfect lips, which meant some poor woman was wearing lips that looked like two boards sliding together when she smiled.

"It isn't just you," she added. "I do not remember my own mother, either."

Again, there wasn't a speck of surprise in his expression.

"'Tis a shame, that. You remind me of her; fiery red hair, eyes the color of autumn leaves, and a face men would go to war for."

An unwelcomed blush heated her cheeks, shocking her. She'd been offered words of flattery before but, for some damnable reason, the words felt warmer, truer coming from Thorn's lips.

Her chest constricted at this new sensation.

"What was her name? Who was she?" The questions tumbled from her lips.

He chuckled softly, the sound caressing her ears like soft fingers.

"Mary Christine MacDeargh," Thorn supplied, his gaze turning inward. Rose watched his face as a ghost of a smile softened his expression. "She was born a fierce and loyal Fraser, which meant none were surprised when she fiercely and loyally battled for your chance to marry whomever you wanted. She did not like the idea that you would be married off like a prize."

Overcome with the urge to hug the mother she couldn't remember, Rose smirked. "That explains it," she surmised.

"What?"

"My fierce desire to not get married. To anyone," she answered defiantly.

Thorn frowned, his pretty lips turning down. So, he didn't like her refusal. She shrugged; he didn't have to like it. She hadn't come to find her family just to be leg-shackled to a complete stranger—no matter how attractive he was.

More than attractive; it wasn't just his muscular body, deep voice, and handsome face, there was something about him that drew her.

"You must be tired," he said, pushing up from his seat to tower over her, his eyes dark and unreadable.

"Aye, I could sleep," she remarked, standing as well, not once looking away.

"I will have Briar come to your chamber in the morning, to look in on you." As he spoke, his expression darkened.

She wanted to throw her head back and laugh; in that moment, she realized that *he* realized he was in a bind. He'd just claimed Rose as his long-lost betrothed, yet he already had a betrothed, one that smelled of dead rose petals.

"Aye," she chirped. "Briar."

Thorn grunted, his black brows turned down as lines etched into grooves beside his eyes.

Without another word, Thorn moved to the wall where a rope hung and he pulled it.

Moments later, the man named Garrick arrived.

"Escort our guest to the room Marbeth prepared," Thorn ordered. He turned back to Rose as Garrick stopped just outside the door, offering them another moment of privacy. "We will discuss this in greater detail tomorrow. I have many more questions for you, and I know you will have questions for me." He stopped, running his hand through his hair, which mussed it terribly. "You have come home, Rose. For now, we will set aside talk of our betrothal, but do not mistake me, we *will* come back to it, and you will give me a chance to fulfil my father's desire to tie our families together."

Their families?

She had no family. And now, more than ever before, she felt the loss of them.

CHAPTER 10

Lord, if he never saw another tome of clan history again, it would be too soon.

After watching Rose depart the study the night before, Thorn had thrown himself into his father's collection of family records, looking for any information he could find about the MacDearghs. Finding the MacPherson connection to the MacDearghs was easy, but finding any details about what happened to the MacDearghs after Angus died was difficult. It was almost as if his father had lost all interest in continuing to archive anything to do with the MacDearghs.

From his own memories, he knew the MacDearghs were a clan farther in the north, in the harsher wilderness, but they were a good, hardworking, and peaceful people. Unfortunately, they were reclusive, seeking to remain apart from the other clans, especially after their one attempt to form an alliance with a southern clan had turned tragic.

It wasn't until the first morning light had turned the sky from black to gray that he ventured to his bedchamber to get a few hours of sleep.

Throwing his legs over the edge of his bed, Thorn rubbed the sleepless grit from his eyes, moaning. He stretched, rolling his shoulders to rid them of the stiffness that his restlessness had wrought.

With so much about Rose left to uncover; what she'd been doing for twenty-one years, what she'd been doing for the smuggling Rees, and where she laid her loyalties, he knew it was best to keep the truth of her identity hidden.

At first, he'd been wary about leaving Rose to Briar's ministrations that morning, but he realized that, as against the idea of their betrothal as she was, Rose wouldn't say a word about it. And he was thankful. He couldn't imagine what Briar would do if she discovered that he was preparing to call off their wedding.

And damn, he felt like an arse for forgetting about their upcoming wedding during his time with Rose. He'd been so shocked when he'd realized who she was that all other thoughts had fled his mind. He'd focused on Rose, who she was, and what it meant now that she had returned.

Once he'd remembered that he had promised to marry Briar just the week before, an invisible boulder plummeted into his belly.

Groaning, he pressed the heels of his palms into his eyes, welcoming the pain. His elbows dug into the top of his knees as he held the weight of his own head. His own thoughts.

Before his failed attempts to rest the night before, he'd told Garrick about what he'd learned. Understandably, Garrick was both shocked and wary. He reminded Thorn that many of the schemers that had come before had seemed credible, and Thorn agreed with him, but then he revealed the one piece of evidence that none of the other women even knew about. The birthmark on the left arse cheek. He'd only known about it because he'd caught Little Rose swimming without a stitch on when she was no more than four years old. He'd laughed at her about it then tattled on her. After that, she'd refused to even look at him, she was so enraged.

Aye...that was the Little Rose he remembered, a scorching temper that matched her hair.

But that was so long ago, and Rose had grown into a woman who did a much better job keeping her temper in check; he'd barely seen a hint of it the night before, though he could readily sense that there was more to her, buried deep beneath the smirks and unbanked desire in her eyes.

Once Thorn had told Garrick about the mark on Rose's arse and how he was convinced that she was his true betrothed, Garrick snickered and then groaned. "I dinnae envy ye, I cannae believe that Briar will take it happily..." he'd said, shuddering.

Was it wise to tell anyone about Rose? He knew Rose was skittish and had rejected the idea of their engagement, but...what if he could convince her? What if he could get her to stay, to marry him, to grace his bed with her beautiful, lush body? It would take some doing, certainly, and he knew that if everyone else knew the truth of her identity, she would run for the hills. She came to Kinloch Rannoch to learn about her history, her family, and he could give that to her, but it would be difficult to go about showing her both a reason to stay and her reason for coming in the first place if they were inundated by the curious, the well-wishers, and the doubters.

Then again, if he didn't tell Briar, she would continue planning their wedding, a wedding he was now, more than ever, convinced was a bad idea. He never should have settled for someone simply to put an end to his self-made problems. It wasn't fair to Briar. Or himself.

Nay, Briar wasn't who he wanted.

Rose....

A vision of red hair held tightly in his fist as he pounded his shaft in between two pale, plump arse cheeks made his manhood harden. He was naked, preferred to sleep that way, and so his erect flesh was there, begging for his hand to offer a release.

But it would be short-lived and unfulfilling.

Groaning, Thorn left the bed, his bare feet slapping against the cold stone floor as he made his way to the wash stand. He made short work of his morning toilet and then dressed in his tartan with his leather breeches beneath. He was sliding his boots on when there came a knock on his door.

Sighing, not ready to make conversation with whoever was at the door, he hesitated. When the knock came again, he straightened, damned if he would allow himself to shirk his responsibilities, no matter how tiresome or vexing they were.

"Come," he called, standing and drawing his shoulders back.

The door latch clicked and the door swung open, and the last person he thought to see stuck her head in, spying him across the room and nearly knocking him on his arse with a smile so blinding he swore he saw stars.

"Rose," he grumbled, finally finding his voice. "What brings you to my bedchamber?"

Without answering him, she slid into the room, quickly shutting the door behind her.

She stopped just before him and he couldn't quite fathom what he was seeing.

There, in front of him, Rose was wearing...a dress. But not just any dress, one made using the MacPherson tartan. The red, deep blue, black with gold and white pinstripes were well known to him, having seen them all his life. But never had they looked as stunning as they did in that moment, draped over Rose Rees. Nay! Rose MacDeargh.

The woman he *would* marry—if fate would ever give him a chance at happiness.

How can you be so willing to marry now after all the schemers that made your blood run cold? When the woman who bested five of his men and strode into his life had set his blood on fire with a single glance.

"Why are you staring at me like that?" she interrupted his troubled and yet eye-opening thoughts.

"You are wearing the MacPherson tartan," he replied, moving to the side board beside the window to pour himself much needed dram of whiskey.

From behind him, she huffed. "Are you going to share? I would not mind a little fortification after what I have already faced this day."

"Problems?" he inquired, curious about everything to do with her.

She grunted adorably. "Aye. Your betrothed sought to attend me during my ablutions, all the while stabbing me to death with her eyes."

Turning, Thorn handed her the tumbler he'd poured for himself. She threw the burning liquid back and groaned, her eyes closed and her face flushed.

Suddenly, that image combined with another, of her poised over him, her naked breasts swaying as she ground her hips against his, riding him to their mutual ecstasy.

Her eyes popped open and she pinned him with eyes the color of mead, swirling with heat and hunger. Had she somehow heard his thoughts, seeing what he envisioned? Did she feel what he felt whenever they were together? Hell, even when they were apart, he'd thought of her, and it had only been the one night since they'd met. What sort of agony would he feel enduring more nights like that? He'd have bollocks as hard and aching as if they'd been frozen and then slowly thawed. Aye, agony.

Clearing his throat, he asked, "What else do you believe you'll encounter today that has you drinking my whiskey?"

She handed him the tumbler and he poured two fingers for himself, sipping it as she waited for her answer.

"The woman, Marbeth, who gave me these clothes—" she began scratching at the material gathered around her hips— "told me that there are some people in the village who could tell me more about the MacDearghs."

He had thought about that possibility the night before, then again, with the MacDearghs self-imposed isolation from other clans, he wasn't too sure there were any left in Kinloch Rannoch who could tell her anything.

They would try, though.

Tensing, Thorn inquired, making sure to keep his voice even, "What did *you* tell Marbeth, exactly?"

A red brow curled up, and he recognized that as her tell. She was curious about his curiosity.

"If you are worried that I would inform her about the betrothal rubbish you told me last night, worry not. I would not tell a soul, even if they tortured it from me, pulling out my fingernails, removing my teeth, peeling the skin from my bel—"

"I get it—hell, woman." He tugged his fingers through his hair, before finishing his whiskey. "I only asked because I think it would be easier for you to inquire about your family if you weren't fending off droves of well-wishers and gawkers coming to see the long-lost MacDeargh with their own eyes."

She snorted, again scratching at the material.

"What bothers you?" he asked, pointing to where she was practically tearing into the material.

Grunting, she answered, "I am not accustomed to having so much...wool this close to my skin. 'Tis like wearing a briar bush on my hips." Again, she scratched then threw her hands into the air and growled. "I would much rather wear my breeches, but I figured that since I am here to learn about my family, 'tis best for me to not draw unwanted attention to myself."

He nodded, understanding her reasoning, and agreeing with it wholeheartedly.

"And what about your sword?" He could feel his eyes crinkling at the sides as he fought the grin that tugged at his cheeks. "Will you hide it beneath the skirts?"

Unamused, she flayed his face with burning eyes. "Do I need my sword, my lord?"

Oh, the menace rising from her, thrumming in that single question. He had never seen Rose wield a sword, but he would wager his left arm that she was dangerous. Hell, five of his men had come home bloody and bruised, and she looked as fresh as if she'd just strolled through a garden in the spring.

"Nay. You are safe here, Rose," he intoned, infusing his voice with a threat of his own...against any who dared to harm her.

She planted her hands on her hips, eyeing him warily before nodding curtly.

"If I am to remain here, who shall we tell others I am? I am still unconvinced that I am this Rosette MacDeargh, though I am willing to speak to the villagers. If I am to know the truth without doubt, I must uncover it myself."

"The easiest thing would be to introduce you as Rose Owains, come from Wales to visit with me after our many years together as children."

Rose cocked her head, her eyes wide.

"You mentioned that last night, about fostering with a Welsh family..." she drawled.

"Aye," he answered, though he was not yet prepared to share that part of his life with her. "But there's no time to discuss that. We must break our fast, and then I can take you into the village and you can ask all the questions you want."

If her smile at greeting him had been blinding, the one she gave him now outshone the sun a million times over.

"What are we waiting for?" she snapped excitedly as she turned for the door, threw it open, and disappeared through it. "Pick up your feet, Thorn, I've a life to get on with!" Her words taunted him, even as a grin spread across his face.

CHAPTER 11

If Rose could bottle the hatred on the face of the woman seated across from her, she'd make a fortune selling it as a weapon.

She ignored Briar as much as she could, but since the woman never seemed to look away from Rose, Rose had to stomach eating her meal with the feeling of being burned alive with a gaze.

The food was good enough, filling if a little bland, but she didn't care what she ate as long as Thorn kept his promise to take her into the village.

"Tell me again, how this woman came tae our doorstep," Briar sneered, her imperious expression cutting nicks in Rose's carefully built wall. The wall meant to keep Briar safe from Rose's temper.

She's lucky I left my sword under my pillow, she mentally grumbled, doing everything she could to not sneer at Briar in return. What did the woman have against Rose? It wasn't as though Rose had come to take Thorn from her, on the contrary, she was happy to leave Thorn in Briar's capable hands, because if he was too busy with his bride-to-be, then he wouldn't be around to drive Rose mad with the way her body responded to a simple look.

Damn him and his dark, devastatingly sensual eyes. And his lips should be a crime*!*

Thorn was at the head of the long table, set on a dais at the back of the great hall, and every one of his men—it seemed that way anyway—were all seated at other long tables in the room. And now, they were all turned to stare at them with interest and suspicion in their weathered and scarred faces.

"I have come from Wales to visit with your laird," she answered, leaning back in her seat to appear unbothered by all the unwanted attention. Usually, she liked being the focus of men's attentions, it made it easier to crook a finger and get them into her bed, a quick and easy way to numb the world for a few hours. But, here, in Thorn's great hall, she wanted to pry out the eyes of everyone present and drop them onto the floor where they'd step on them in their panic to escape her.

She choked on a laugh at the vision that conjured, but reset her features as Thorn's gaze landed on her.

"Aye, Rose Owains is an old friend, and she is here to offer condolences for my father's passing," Thorn commented, and Rose wanted to kick him under the table. The man couldn't lie his way out of an arm-wrestling match with a babe.

Briar scowled. "After four years?" she shrilled. "Do ye take me for an idiot?"

Rose cocked her head as if to say, "Aye," but she kept that to herself. Instead, she decided to clean up the mess Thorn had made of the situation.

"The Owains are busy, and we rarely, if ever, come close enough to Scotland to hear any news of Thorn or the MacPherson clan. The only reason I knew about his father's passing was because I had met with two men in Port Eynon Bay who'd mentioned it. As the only Owains available, I was sent north on behalf of the family, to offer our sympathies."

Thorn's face remained impassive, but his eyes twinkled with unspoken amazement.

Her chest swelled, pride pulsing through her at that look. How long had it been since someone looked at her like that?

Too long.

"I see," Briar intoned, with a sour turn of her lips. "And how long will ye be stayin' with us...Rose?" A sick sort of joy crawled through her, and Rose let that sensation pick her next words.

"I will stay as long as Laird MacPherson allows it. He has already shown such...*hospitality*," she said, emphasizing the last word, and cocking her lips in a lopsided smile.

Briar gasped, Garrick choked on whatever he was eating, and Thorn stared at her like she'd grown a second head. She wanted to laugh at them all, then laugh at herself for allowing her emotions to rule her mind.

"And by that, I mean that he has allowed me to stay, and has provided me with the proper attire befitting a lady. If he had not, I'd be sleeping with my horse on those bloody moors, and I would be well on my way to dead by exposure."

Briar grunted, Garrick smirked into his mug of ale, and Thorn tried his damnedest to hide the smirk on his own face behind a frown.

Opening her mouth to speak, Briar was immediately interrupted by Thorn's loud, authoritative voice. "Rose will stay here as long as she likes, and we will continue to be hospitable to her. She is a guest, in this house and in this country, and we will do what we can to show her that the MacPhersons are the best damn clan in all of Scotland."

A rousing shout of "here, here" rose up, and many more voices followed, until the great hall was vibrating with the noise.

Cringing, Rose nearly missed the look of absolute hatred that blackened Briar's face, but it disappeared the moment Thorn spoke again.

"Garrick, you will accompany myself and Rose into the village, she would like to take in the sights."

Briar shot to her feet, a storm cloud hovering over her head. "My love, should I no' accompany ye as well, as our weddin' is approachin', I find myself in need o' a few things."

Thorn wanted to turn her down, Rose could read it on his face and in his stiffened posture, but Garrick did it for him.

"'Tis better for ye tae remain here tae look after the needs o' the men who're comin' in from their patrols in the north. They will need food and mayhaps nursin' back tae health."

Briar opened her mouth, no doubt to protest, but Thorn agreed. "I can trust no one else to the task, Briar," Thorn offered coaxingly, and the scowling woman's face fell.

Within the quarter hour, Garrick, Thorn, and Rose were mounted on their respective horses—Rose was glad to see her brave and handsome Martle again—and they were trotting out through the gates along the wide dirt road toward the village in the distance.

Unused to riding a horse while wearing so much fabric, Rose had needed assistance mounting, and when Garrick arrived to aid her, she dashed away the sharp disappointment that is wasn't Thorn whose hand cradled her arse as she fumbled her way to sitting astride in a goddamn skirt!

As with every hurdle in her life, Rose learned quickly, and soon she was riding in between Thorn and Garrick as if she'd been riding in fabric shackles made of wool all her life.

They spoke little on the journey into town expect for the few attempts at conversation that Garrick had thrown. She gave one word answers, Thorn did the same, and eventually Garrick gave up. It wasn't a long ride, anyway, and within a half hour, they were entering the village proper.

Will anyone here have what I am looking for? Will they know anything about my father...my mother? Me? If the laird of the MacDearghs was such close friends with Thorn's father, surely there were some in the village who would remember him.

As they entered the village, small groups of people came to meet their laird, smiling up at him and raising their hands in greeting. Many of them stared at her, questions filling their eyes, but none of them spoke with her or spoke to Thorn about her. And she didn't mind that. She didn't want to have to lie and clean up another one of

Thorn's slips, though, she wondered if the blunder at the table that morning hadn't been intentional.

Dismounting, Thorn tossed his reins to a young lad, no older than her cousin Brendan's adopted boys, and came around to her right side. He gazed up at her, his lips quirking mischievously...sensually. Damn his perfect lips!

"Here, let me help you down," he drawled, reaching up to grasp her around the waist.

A shock of heat and awareness blasted through her, and her breath caught. Thorn's eyes widened and his pupils shrank in shock. Did that mean he felt that, too?

Scooting forward, Rose allowed Thorn to pull her into his chest. He held her there for one, two, three, four beats, before loosening his hold so she could slide down the length of him, her breasts crushed against him, her nipples hard as they brushed his hardness.

A groan, deep and wicked, escaped his throat, and Rose groaned in return, the heat between them rising to surround them fully, as if to shut out the world around them, and cocoon them in their desire for one another.

Garrick cleared his throat and Thorn released his hold on her, and Rose wished—not for the first time that day—that she had her sword with which to gut someone.

Scowling at Garrick from over her shoulder, Rose tossed Martle's reins to a waiting lad who was staring at her agog. What? Had he never seen a woman in a tartan before? She pondered her appearance; she'd left her hair unbraided, and it probably looked a fright after their ride into the village, but that couldn't be why the boy was peering at her so.

Thorn leaned in until his mouth nearly touched her ear. "He thinks you are beautiful."

Stunned warmth shot through her, a tingling heat that blazed from her ear where his hot breath fluttered over her flesh.

"Beautiful?" she repeated, still uncertain if that was the look on the boy's face.

"Aye," Thorn asserted. "And I agree with him. As beautiful as any woman has a right to be."

His dark eyes burned down into hers, like black fire engulfing the depths of him. He must have seen an answering desire in her own eyes because his mouth drew into a line and his nostrils flared, making Rose's own body vibrate with anticipation.

"The most beautiful rose in the world," he whispered huskily.

This time, at his words, the heat that blazed through her built from her belly outward, her womanhood pulsing with an ache she recognized as one she hadn't felt in much too long. Attraction, deep and shocking. Aye, she'd been called beautiful many times before but…she hadn't believed a word of it, until now.

Until Thorn.

Damn, she was walking right into trouble…and she couldn't be more excited.

CHAPTER 12

MacDougal pressed the lit taper against the wick of the red prayer candle in the narthex. Just like every afternoon, he came to offer his prayers to the Holy Virgin, and his supplications to the Archangel Michael to bring about holy justice against those who'd wronged him. Wronged his family. Stole his son's life.

There, in the quiet stillness of the chapel, his memories crept in, intent on haunting him once more.

"MacDougal.... There has been an accident...." Those words had been the first step to his ruin. To the ruin of his family, of his clan.

"Where is my boy?" he'd asked, knowing that Bruce had gone riding with the eldest MacPherson boy and their foster, a Welsh lad named Dafydd, but his son had not yet returned, and the night had grown dark. "Where is my boy?" he'd bellowed, but the look on the guard's face told him what his mouth had feared to say.

"What has happened tae him?" he'd demanded, and the guard, a man long dead now, had told him of how MacPherson's boy, Aron, had goaded the other boys into swimming in the river, the same river that had been swollen from days of rain. The Welsh boy was lost first, and then his own beloved Bruce was washed down river. Blasted

Aron MacPherson had been the only one who'd remained ashore—the coward had refused to jump at the very last minute, and onlookers were shocked at what he'd done. It had taken hours to find the bodies, both tucked up under the branches of trees that had fallen into the water, their roots unable to hold when the earth gave way.

"What o' the MacPherson boy?" he'd asked, his unutterable sorrow swiftly darkening into rage.

"We dinnae know. He ran...."

Before his son's body was laid to rest, he'd made it his mission to find and strangle the boy who had cost him his son's life. But—once a coward always a coward—Aron MacPherson was found days later, hanging by his neck from a willow tree. In that moment, MacDougal knew that no matter what it took, he would get his revenge against the MacPhersons because their coward son had stolen that from him as well.

But his revenge was taking longer than he'd hoped. Since the Welsh lad had been lost, in order to make reparations to the family, MacPherson sent his own son to Wales to foster with the late boy's family. In Wales, protected by the fierce Cylldon nobles, Dubhach MacPherson was untouchable. And though Dairmaid MacPherson was close enough to kill in his sleep, MacDougal wanted him to suffer as he had suffered, he wanted him to know what it felt like to lose his son. It would take years to get his revenge, but he'd believed it would be worth it. Then that bastard MacPherson had to die without aid from MacDougal—once again the MacPhersons stole something from him.

For the last time. No more. He would get his vengeance, and it would be sweeter now because once Dubhach MacPherson was gone, MacDougal would take all that was left; the wealth, the land, the legacy, and he would burn it all.

The sounds of pounding hoof beats dragged him from his battered, hideous thoughts.

"We have received word from Gleneden..." Barton announced, his chest heaving from the exertion it took to run from the courtyard to the nave of the family chapel. "MacPherson is headed into Kinloch Rannoch unescorted."

"Thorn never leaves Gleneden, that man never has need. The women flock to his door as if it were a reverse brothel," he sneered.

"Aye, but he is there, in the village. Many have remarked upon it."

"So...he will be travelin' back tae Gleneden before the sun sets." It was a statement, one on which he could build the rest of what he'd been wanting to say for years.

"Take him. Kill any who get in yer way. This night, MacPherson will fall intae my hands."

A thrill burst through his chest, as an idea began to form. Forget slowly burning everything MacPherson loved to the ground, he would take MacPherson, bury him in the dungeons, and watch as he slowly, painfully died in the dark. It would be fitting, since his own son had died in the dark and cold of the river.

"She certainly had much to say," Rose remarked as Thorn closed the door to the cottage in which they'd spent the last three hours. "I have never met someone who knew so little about so much."

Thorn chuckled, grinning down at the woman he simply couldn't stop looking at. During their time in the cottage with old Mrs. Jenkins, he'd watched as she interacted with the woman, accepting the terrible tasting bowl of mutton stew and then the surprisingly tasty tart without a single grimace, and answering the woman's questions even though they'd gone to that particular cottage to get *answers* from the old woman.

Mrs. Jenkins had been a pillar of the village for more than fifty years. She'd been there long before Thorn or his older brother, Aron, were born, and she would still be around long after Thorn was dead. She was as hard to kill as a flea, and just as tiny. But if anyone knew more about the MacDeargh clan, it would have been her. Unfortunately, she knew about as much about what happened to them as Thorn did. Not much.

He'd spent too long in Wales, and he hadn't written to his father often enough. He knew that his father and Angus MacDeargh had been lads together, and he knew that the MacDeargh clan was an off-shoot clan of the MacPhersons. He also knew that, like many other smaller clans, during the famines that had decimated the land, their numbers dwindled. Marrying their children to one another was a desperate attempt to cement the clans, allowing for the isolated MacDearghs to take on the protection of the fierce MacPhersons.

But, after the MacDeargh laird died in that shipwreck, and Thorn's betrothed presumed dead as well, the hopes for weaving the families together were lost. Angus was the last male of his line, and Thorn was now the last of his.

He was duty-bound to marry and beget strong sons to continue the line, which was why he'd agreed to marry Briar—she'd been the least terrible option.

Until Rose had arrived and turned everything upside-down.

Beside him, Rose walked silently, her face cast down in thought.

What is going on inside her head? What was she thinking about that made her beautiful lips pinch together like that?

"What is bothering you?" he asked, pausing to let her shorter legs catch up. She stopped abruptly, nearly colliding with him.

On a huff, she retorted, "Does something have to be bothering me? Can I not just...be?" She threw her hands into the air, nearly whacking him in the face.

"Your face gives you away, Little Rose. I remember how you used to pinch your lips together when you were contemplating mayhem."

Her eyebrows shot up in surprise.

"You remember that?" she asked, and he nodded. "About me?" He nodded again, unable to keep the smile from curling his lips.

"Aye. I remember much about you, Little Rose, but it isn't the little girl I want to know now, 'tis the woman." He reached out, sliding a finger along her cheek. Soft, silky, and flushed with pink.

"There is little to know about me, Thorn. I was lost, now I am found, and in between, I did a little sinning."

"Oh?" he inquired, suddenly very interested in hearing about her sins.

She crossed her arms over her chest, but because of the modest blouse and the thick tartan she wore, her breasts were hidden. Shame. An utter shame.

"I take it you are wondering what sins your lost betrothed has committed," she drawled, her upper lip cocking into a wicked grin.

"Of course, if only to help you repent," he murmured, his voice dropping as he leaned down to get closer to those lips.

Without missing a beat, she leaned in, bringing their lips close enough that he could smell the honey from the tarts they'd just eaten.

"I should be ashamed to admit that I...have committed sins of the flesh."

He swallowed, his bollocks pulling up into his body as his shaft hardened. "Tell me...." God, he was only torturing himself—nay, he was allowing *her* to torture them both.

"I have lain with a man...well, many men, and...."

He wanted to hate that she wasn't an innocent, but he wasn't a hypocritical prude. He had lain with many, *many* women—especially over the last four years, so it wouldn't be fair to think her a whore for doing the same thing. Still, though...he was jealous.

"And?" he prodded, his hands rising to cup her face.

"And what?" she murmured, her brown eyes hazy. She blinked up at him, confusion flirting with the heat of desire in her gaze.

"And...you wish to know what it feels like to lie with me, in my bed, beneath me," he answered for her, his whole body on fire with the promise in his own words.

Something must have happened in her mind because she stiffened before pulling away as if burned.

"Nay, 'tis not possible," she grumbled.

Thorn growled, reaching for her, determined to return to whatever it was that was happening between them.

"You are my betrothed, Rose, we can damn well pleasure one another—"

"Briar," she snapped, pinning him with a cold glower. "You are betrothed to Briar. I have never, not once, lain with a man who belonged to another, and I will not start now. No matter how much I want to."

She whirled, her skirts flying out around her as she strode away, leaving a frustrated and guilty-hearted man in her wake.

CHAPTER 13

After their moment outside Mrs. Jenkin's cottage, Rose did everything she could to turn off the fountain of longing that Thorn had tapped. It didn't help that the scoundrel had made it his personal mission to touch her at every opportunity, brushing against her when they walked, sliding his knee or thigh against hers when they sat to question another villager, and damned if she wasn't enjoying all that touching. And that was the problem. The more time she spent with him, the more she came to realize that he truly and honestly believed her his lost betrothed.

He was considerate, protective—placing the flat of his hand against her lower back to direct her and to show the male villagers that *she* was with *him*. She knew that if it had been anyone else, any other time, she would have broken that hand. But, since it was Thorn, and she liked Thorn's touch—much to her chagrin, she allowed it. The best part, though, was a smile was never far from his face. Save for those moments after her refusal of their mutual pleasure, he had kept up a show of joviality, introducing her to the villagers with a grin, and constantly keeping her laughing.

She hadn't laughed so much—true, honest laughter—in years. In ever, probably.

But no matter how charming and wonderful Thorn was, she could not have what she was beginning to realize she wanted.

A home of her own, a man who treated her as precious in public, but lit her on fire with his touch in private.

I could have that with Thorn. Nay. She might not be a woman of high morals, but she would never cross *that* line, the one that would make her the *other woman*, the woman that tore families apart. As her adopted grandfather had done too many times.

She couldn't remember much about her own parents, but it pleased her to think that they were faithful to one another. Perhaps... if she were to ever marry, she would have a marriage she could pride herself on.

Marry? You? What man would have you, soiled goods. Criminal. It pricked her conscience, even more so that those things had never bothered her until now. Until it mattered what someone else might think of her.

Aye, Thorn believed he wanted her, but that was only because he was determined to marry to fulfil an obligation to two dead men.

It wasn't real. So, she would endure the smiles and the touches, and she would return to her bedchamber at Gleneden, and she would pack her meager belongings and return to the village. There was an inn, and the food looked tasty enough, and she knew the whiskey would be watered down, but she could wrestle the good stuff from the barkeep without too much effort.

Aye, she had a plan now. Now to do it without getting distracted, or allowing Thorn to sway her.

That is easier said than accomplished, Rose.

And what else had she accomplished thus far? She thought about the day, and the lack of information she'd learned about the MacDearghs. It seemed hopeless; how did an entire clan disappear and no one know about it?

Flustered, she stopped mid-stride, and turned to Thorn who was, as always, following along beside her. He drew up close to her, his face hidden in the growing shadows of the falling sun.

"How is it that you do not know what happened to the MacDeargh clan?" she said, sourly. She hated feeling as though she were treading on uneven ground. Never in her life had she been so close to the truth and yet so far. Her parents had spent time in this village, they had been close friends with the former laird of the MacPhersons, so why couldn't she even get a sliver of information from anyone?

Thorn sighed, lifting his arm to run his fingers through his shoulder-length black hair. Rose tried to ignore the way his corded bicep muscle flexed and bunched as he moved.

"There are records in my father's study, and I spent all of last evening poring through them, but there was nothing there that will help us."

"Records? Can I see them?" she asked, hope sliding up on the scale, even a fraction of an inch.

"Aye, you can," he replied.

"And there is nothing you know, nothing you remember about them?" she prodded, unwilling to believe that someone who was to marry into the MacDearghs hadn't learned anything of importance about them.

"I wish I could tell you something, Rose, but, well, I left for Wales at a young age, and I didn't hear from home all that often, and when I did, it was always talk of the house, the villagers, and the less than pleasant dealings with the MacDougals."

MacDougals? It was the first time she'd heard that name, but from the way Thorn's voice dropped, the MacDougals had been trouble for some time.

Focus!

"But, surely, you heard something about what happened after the shipwreck," she pushed, her frustration mounting.

"Nay, I only heard about it, and I mourned for your parents...and for you," he said, his voice soft and yet heavy. Rose noticed that his hands had clenched at his sides, opening and closing, as though he wanted to reach out to her. To comfort her or to stir her, she didn't know.

But I want to....

"But you did not think to ask about the rest of the clan? Perhaps who would take on the mantle of laird after my father had died?"

If she could see his face, she wondered if she'd see guilt or shame coloring his face.

"I was a lad, I did not think about the long-term consequences of your father's loss. I was more interested in riding horses, playing tricks on maids, and exploring the woods outside of Cylldon."

A sense of guilt rushed her; of course, Thorn, as a lad, would think and act as a lad would. She was a fool to think he would care about matters an adult would.

Pressing a hand to her forehead, she let out a slow breath.

"I understand, Thorn, and I am sorry," she offered, a sort of grimace-smile on her face. "I am such a fool—"

Thorn growled. He moved quickly—faster than she'd ever seen—and took her into his arms. Wrapped around her, his arms felt like heaven. Dazed by the sensation, she didn't even think to push him away, and she certainly didn't push him away when his lips crashed down on hers. His kiss was unexpected in that it was softer, gentler, more coaxing. She leaned into him, welcoming the warmth of his body, the blazing heat of his mouth on hers, and the slow building comfort she hadn't known she needed.

But Thorn had.

ROSE, IN HIS ARMS, HER TASTE IN HIS MOUTH, HAD BEEN BETTER than any fantasy he'd ever had.

And he was determined to taste more, to experience more, to touch and devour more.

She was the sweetest, tartest, most delicious woman he had ever tasted, and in a second, he'd become addicted to her. He would have her. Forever. As his wife. Damn anyone who got in his way.

Thorn couldn't stop the tingling in his lips, nor the pulsing in his groin, nor the need to gallop home, steal Rose upstairs to his chamber, and not let her leave until he'd made her come a dozen times. Until neither of them could walk, and she had agreed to become his wife.

Shortly after they departed the village, Rose and Garrick began bantering back and forth, Garrick was sharing stories of his younger sister, Marbeth, and Rose would laugh and ask questions, and make short yet shallow comments. Since their kiss, Rose had seemed less engaged, as though she wasn't all there.

And neither was he. He couldn't focus, couldn't think, couldn't make his body settle down.

He could understand why she was withdrawn; she'd apparently wasted a whole day asking questions about a clan no one could speak about.

There has to be more out there, there has to be something someone is not telling. Perhaps he would send a company of men north to Dearghrose Castle. He'd have them deliver a letter reporting the return of the former laird's daughter. They would rejoice, wouldn't they? They'd send someone to Gleneden, wouldn't they? Who better to tell her about her parents than someone who knew them personally?

Why haven't I thought of that before? Because he'd been so caught up in Rose, in who she was to him, that he didn't consider what she would want or need, like details about her people. The people who made her who she was. Her blood.

As they continued on the wide dirt road, sounds in the lines of trees on each side made the hairs on his neck stand erect.

Thorn opened his mouth to tell Garrick to be aware but before the words could leave his lips a blood-curdling screech filled the air just before darkly dressed men poured from the covering boughs and into the road, cutting off their progress and their retreat.

The horses screamed as Thorn, Garrick, and Rose pulled on their reins. Alarm shot through him, and Thorn immediately turned to check on Rose.

She was seated on her saddle, her face pale and her expression grim, but there was a welcomed and somewhat surprising flash of pure anger in her eyes. Aye, his lass was a spirited and fierce woman —she had bested five of his men on her own. Then again, he doubted his men were fighting to hurt her; though they were battle-hardened men, they were also husbands and fathers, and they wouldn't have truly harmed Rose.

But these men, brandishing swords and sneers, they would hurt her for the fun of it.

Not if I kill them first!

Pulling his sword from the scabbard tied to his saddle, he dismounted in a single movement, landing on his feet with a shout. Garrick appeared beside him, his sword raised.

"Dammit!" Rose yelled and Thorn turned to spy her trying to get off her horse. Her skirts tangled around her legs as she kicked to free herself from them.

Before he could tell her to remain where she was, the men who'd flooded from the woods attacked. Two against eight—the odds were deadly.

Raising he sword, Thorn delivered a stinging blow to the sword of the first man to advance. The sword broke in half from the impact. Stunned, the man dropped the broken piece from his hand and stepped back, right into Garrick's swing. That man was dead before his head rolled from his shoulders.

One down, seven to go. Damn!

"Ha!" A feminine voice cried, but before Thorn could look to see what had happened, another two men advanced. Struggling against the force of two men, Thorn fought to catch his breath, his heart racing.

He saw her then...Rose was warring beside Garrick. While Thorn was busy fighting, she had dismounted, picked up the broken sword the first man dropped, and was easily holding her own against two men. God how he wanted to watch her fight, her movements graceful and yet brutal, but he had his own problems to deal with.

With the three of them fighting, the fight was over much sooner than Thorn had expected. He could only assume that the men weren't trained fighters because up against Thorn, Garrick, and the surprisingly skilled Rose, they did not stand a chance.

Sheathing his sword, Thorn strode to the only man left alive.

"Who sent you?" Thorn demanded, wrapping his hand around the bastard's throat. He could feel the man swallowing, his body trembling as the warmth of his own blood fled his body through the slash in his side. "Who sent you?" he demanded again.

The man's eyes grew wide then slid closed. Thorn shook him, damned if he let he man die before he got his answers.

"Ma-MacDougal," the man sputtered, blood dribbling from the corners of his mouth.

That name rocked Thorn back on his heels. MacDougal sent these men? But why?

Thorn shook the man again. "*Why* did he send you?"

"Ca...capture...."

"What?" That wasn't answer enough, there was still too much left unsaid. "Explain!"

A wet gasp escaped the man's chest before he fell limp against Thorn.

Damn! Damn! Damn!

Rolling the man's body to the ground, Thorn stood, wiping the blood from his hands on the dead man's own tunic.

Garrick came up beside him, his chest heaving from having put down three men of his own.

"MacDougal? Why would be send mercenaries to capture you?" he asked, his face ashen.

Thorn spat, his great body vibrating with unspent rage.

"I do not know, but I aim to find out."

The loud thud sounded from behind them and they both spun to find Rose standing over a dead body. She was kicking it and cursing under her breath.

"Rose!" Thorn shouted, hurrying to her side. "Are you injured?" His gaze scanned her for any sign of wounds even as his hands skated over her arms, neck, back, and head. God, he wanted to pull her into his arms and just feel her, to physically experience the rise and fall of her chest, to know, in the very pit of his being, that she was alive. She was breathing.

"Nay, I am not injured, but this bastard—" she kicked the body again— "tore Marbeth's tartan!"

Of all the concerns he expected to hear after a life or death battle —three against eight—he had not expected anger at a dead man for tearing a piece of clothing. His gaze caught on the tear she'd mentioned; it was a ragged rip down the left side, which allowed a teasing showing of long, womanly leg.

She huffed, dropping the sword she'd so expertly wielded onto the ground beside her boot.

Despite all that had just happened, she wasn't acting as he expected a woman to act, then again, she was Rose Rees MacDeargh, daughter of two fierce, hardy clans, raised by the most cunning of smugglers, she would never act, think, or be like other women.

And he was damn grateful for that.

She'd just killed two men with a broken sword, jumping into battle with a shout of excitement and a blinding grin. God, she was glorious, absolutely breathtaking.

He stared at Rose, the pink in her cheeks, the glitter in her eyes, and tension in her stance, and he knew that she was the woman fated for him.

Mine.

CHAPTER 14

By the time they returned to the castle, Rose's whole body felt weighted down with cannon balls tied around her limbs, and her head was spinning, spinning, twisting and turning—who were those men?

She'd heard Garrick and Thorn discussing a man named MacDougal. Who was MacDougal and why had he sent men to capture Thorn?

Removing what was left of Marbeth's tartan, Rose ventured to the wardrobe where several loose tunics hung. She removed one, slipped it on over her head, and tried to untangle the knots from her hair. Fighting always made her hair a nest, which was why she so often wore it in a braid.

A knock on her door made her pause, but her heart continued going, increasing in its tempo, because she knew who was on the other side.

Her hands still in her hair, she walked to the door and said, "Come in."

Thorn opened the door, and she held her breath as he strode in, his gaze on her.

She glanced down, quickly realizing that she was wearing less then than she ever had in his presence, but she wasn't ashamed of her lack of clothing. So it wasn't shame that was making her body turn to liquid fire.

"I told her..." he broke the heavy silence with those three words, and Rose didn't need him to elaborate. She knew exactly who "her" was and what he told her.

"I see," she replied, pulling her suddenly trembling fingers from her hair. She swung the loose hair over her shoulder, brushing rebellious strands from her cheeks. "And what does that have to do with me?"

His dark eyes pierced her, they were hooded as a hawk spying its prey. There was a smoldering there that made all sense flee, not that she'd had much to begin with, not when she had wanted him so badly for so long.

"If Briar is no longer your betrothed...should I feel sympathy for her?"

His gaze traveled over her face, searching for something.

"Only if you wish her to have what I am offering to you instead," he answered, his deep voice thick.

"And what are you offering me?" she asked, her blood racing as tingles of awareness zig-zagged up and down her back.

Instead of answering her immediately, Thorn marched to her, wrapped his arms around her and pulled her into his chest. Her breasts, swollen with anticipation, were crushed against him. She shuddered, the delicious sensation of her nipples rubbing against the rough fabric of her woolen tunic sending hot want into the crease between her thighs.

"I am offering you everything," he growled, bending down to capture her lips. She gasped as something hard and large pressed into her belly.

Flushed, her body screaming for release, she stood on her tiptoes, taking control of their kiss as she'd wanted to since earlier that day.

And he gave as good as he got—even more so—fulfilling her deepest most sensual needs.

And her every longing.

~

"WHAT?" MACDOUGAL BELLOWED, SLAMMING HIS FIST INTO the already scarred surface of his table. "What dae ye mean they are all dead?" His voice was raised, his heart pounding, as he listened to Barton repeat what he'd said moments ago.

"When none o' the men returned tae the bolt hole, I went tae check...." Barton's face turned green then red again. "They were all dead, butchered. I have never seen such viciousness in an attack before."

"Ye said there were only three o'them—*three*! And one o' them a woman! How do two men kill eight?"

"I cannae say," Barton admitted, his lips pressed into a thin line.

His blood thickening as bile coated his tongue, MacDougal spat.

"Bring his wench here, she has much tae answer for."

Barton tensed, eyeing MacDougal carefully. "My laird...I dinnae know if that will matter."

He huffed impatiently. "What? Dinnae speak in riddles, ye daft git, I havenae the patience for it!"

"In the village, there were some who spied the MacPherson with another woman. A woman with red hair, wearing the MacPherson tartan. He introduced her as Owains. And they were pettin' one another."

MacDougal snorted. "What man doesna have a whore on the side, Barton? What does this have tae do with anythin'?"

"The woman...she was askin' 'round 'bout the MacDearghs," Barton replied, his voice heavy with unspoken portent. "And there were many who didnae believe MacPherson about her bein' an Owains. Whenever he mentioned her surname, she flinched, as though she were unused tae it."

"A red-headed wench askin' round 'bout the MacDearghs, ye say?" It couldn't be, it was impossible.... But was it? Perhaps the Lord has seen fit to provide MacDougal one more piece to add to his unfolding plan.

"Send for the Welshman," MacDougal sneered, a hateful glee filling him. "We'll put his skills tae use as soon as can be arranged, and by the end o' the fortnight, the MacPherson and his whore will be rottin' corpses."

Twelve days had passed since that night they were attacked...and they'd first ravished one another. And every night since, they'd fallen into bed together, enjoying the pleasure they would bring one another, and it was absolute heaven. But Thorn could not ignore the prickle of unease that had been growing into an outright stabbing in his chest. For every moment spent with Rose, there was a sense of foreboding that would spoil the nearly perfect experience.

She was everything he ever thought he wanted in a mate; beautiful, intelligent, fierce, and breathtakingly passionate in bed. She was as insatiable as he was, often tearing at his tartan to get to his naked skin, and sometimes they hadn't even removed all of their clothes before he was inside of her, plunging into utter bliss as he groaned in ecstasy and she cried out his name.

Aye, heaven. And despite the stubborn woman's insistence that they were not betrothed, he continued to hope that she would see reason, that she would find something in him worth keeping.

Lying beside her, after another bed-shaking round of tupping, he grinned at her incessant questions, knowing it was time to tell her all.

"Fine, I will tell you about fostering with the Owains," he replied, tucking her head against his chest so he could play with the tendrils of hair that tickled his belly.

"Then go on, tell me," she said, beaming up at him.

God, he would never get over how beautiful she was.

Clearing his throat, he responded, "I had an older brother, Aron. He died when I was thirteen—"

"And I would have been four," she interjected correctly.

"Aye."

"How did he die?"

Thorn, knowing the pain would come, sighed heavily. "There was an accident. Two boys lost their lives and Aron took the blame for it.... He hung himself."

Rose gasped, her lovely face gone pale. Tears made her eyes glimmer as she stared at him with shock and sorrow on her face.

"I am sorry," she whispered, her breath warm against his chest. He closed his eyes, drinking in the sensation of having her soft curves pressed against him, comforting now even though it had been stirring before.

"'Twas a long time ago. As it was, one of the lads who died was the son of the Lord Owains, who had sent his son to Gleneden to foster with my father, a man who had saved his life during a voyage to Spain when they were both lads themselves. Feeling responsible for the lad's death, my father agreed to send me to Wales, to the Owains, to foster there as sort of a penance for what had happened. I remained there until my father died four year ago."

"And your search for your betrothed began in earnest," she drawled, her voice flat.

"Aye, it did. And I found her," he remarked, not missing the way she stiffened, pulling herself away from him.

Every discussion they'd had about her remaining at Gleneden would often dissolve into an argument, but those arguments always turned into the most earth-shattering sex he'd ever experienced. But everything was like that with Rose, there was never a moment of wasted emotion or sensation or thought. She brought out the best and worst in him, and he was grateful for that. She'd become what he'd needed most after his father's death...the peace he'd never thought to know. With her, he was happy.

But hell was clawing at his happiness, he could feel it, but he couldn't put a finger on what *it* was.

Not wanting to argue just then, though, Thorn wrapped his arms around her naked form and held her against him. They remained like that for long, silent moments, until she fell to sleep, her soft snores making his smile despite the troubling thoughts starting to fill his mind.

Since breaking off things with Briar, the castle hadn't run as smoothly as it usually did; Briar had drawn into herself, only venturing out into the common areas for meals. Thorn was saddened because he'd disappointed someone he genuinely cared about—just not in the way she had wanted him to. He'd known Briar for too long, and while his body had been attracted to her, everything else about him had been resigned to marriage simply because she had been the only choice that hadn't turned his stomach completely.

Now, though, the only choice he could ever consider making was between seducing Rose into marriage or finding something else to tempt her with. Either way, she would be his wife.

She could rebel against what was between them only so long before she gave in. And he would be there, arms wide open.

CHAPTER 15

"When did this come?" Thorn bellowed, lifting and shaking the missive in his hand as Garrick and his other men stared on.

Garrick answered, "George said it was hung from the gate with a dagger—"

"I found it this morn, when I went outside tae check the perimeter," George finished the report, his voice carrying through the great hall from where he was standing by the door. He looked ready to flee under Thorn's rage.

"And has anyone checked her chambers?" Thorn inquired, his voice like ice and fire, cold yet still hot with discontent.

Garrick shifted, lifting his chin. "I checked as soon as I read the missive, my laird. She isnae there, and the room looks torn tae shreds."

A bitter bile rose into Thorn's throat and he spat.

"I must do as MacDougal demands..." though he loathed that very thought of it with every breath in his body.

Garrick growled, his familiar face hardening into a florid mask of disgust.

"Nay, Thorn! Gather the men, we will tear down MacDougal's walls. We will make him rue the day he thought tae take undue action against the MacPhersons!"

Rose cursed, coming to stand beside Thorn, her hand wrapped around his arm and he immediately felt the calm, the peace that came with her touch—when not in the bedchamber.

"But the missive said that he was to come alone or MacDougal would kill her and hang her corpse from the battlements as a sign of your betrayal to the clans."

"Damn that! The man has lost his mind. More than likely, he will kill her anyway, just tae hurt whoever he can. He has hated the MacPhersons for as long as I can remember—"

"Why?" Rose's question seemed to throw Garrick off-kilter. "What could the MacPhersons have possibly done to arouse such malice in one man?"

As though someone had reached into his chest to squeeze his heart, Thorn felt it shudder, struggling to pump through the overwhelming grief that slammed into him.

MacDougal blamed the MacPhersons for something that was as tragic to Thorn as it was to MacDougal. But the man had obviously broken and, if the wound in his heart *had* healed, it hadn't healed right. Though he'd been gone for twenty-two years since the event that devastated them both, Thorn had heard rumors of MacDougal's constant threats, his machinations to destroy any of MacPherson's allies, and his focus on making "all those bloody MacPhersons pay...." Thorn couldn't understand the man's unwavering focus on something that had happened so long ago, and he certainly couldn't understand why MacDougal blamed all MacPhersons for what happened to his son.

Aye, it was terrible and it shouldn't have happened at all, but MacDougal hadn't been the only one to lose someone that day, and yet he couldn't see past his own grief. His own twisted need for revenge.

Because MacDougal had been relatively silent over the last four years since Thorn's father's death, Thorn had been fool enough to think the trouble was done. Apparently, MacDougal had simply been lying in wait, probably for any sign of weakness. A fiancée was a weakness, even though Briar was no longer his betrothed. Not that it mattered—she was still his responsibility, her safety his duty as her laird.

Swallowing to wet his suddenly parched throat, Thorn finally replied, "'Tisn't the time to discuss it. We have only three hours with which to shore up the castle defenses in the event that MacDougal succeeds in his plan to kill me. I have no doubt that, once I am dead, he will turn his wrath toward Gleneden." He knew what that damn missive said, he'd read it a hundred times it seemed, but every time he considered doing as MacDougal demanded, his lips would twist into a sneer and the urge to roar climbed up his backbone. But he had to, he couldn't take the chance. If even there was the slightest hope that Briar could be saved, he had to do whatever he could to ensure her safety.

But what of Rose? his heart cried. What would happen to her? If he did, indeed, die that eve, would she remain at Gleneden, or would she return to Wales, to the Rees? The very thought of Rose leaving made his blood run cold. Nay, she couldn't go, and he refused to die—they had only just begun their lives together.

Oh, aye, she had continued to refuse his offer of marriage, citing that she could never be a laird's bride, but he knew she had it in her to be a loyal, compassionate, and fiery Lady MacPherson. And that wasn't all...he knew there was something else she wasn't telling, another piece of the puzzle he hadn't found yet, the piece that would open her heart and let him in.

"THORN?" ROSE'S SOFTLY PRODDING VOICE INTERRUPTED HIS thoughts, and he peered down into her upturned face. There was worry in her lovely eyes, worry for him, and it made his heart swell. If she worried for him, perhaps there was something there between them he could build on.

"If we dinnae march in, what are we supposed tae do, Thorn?" Garrick asked, his tone telling Thorn that he didn't like not marching in. "We cannae do nothin'."

"Nay, we cannot march in but we can prepare for any retaliatory action against us. We send men to the walls, triple the patrols, and make sure the men remain alert for any trouble. I will go, just as he wanted, but I refuse to leave Gleneden vulnerable," Thorn intoned.

The men all nodded, the group thrumming with anxiety, the need to move, to go, to put blade to throat—though the latter would only occur if MacDougal was foolish enough to attack them. There were hundreds of MacPherson warriors to the several dozen MacDougals, but that wouldn't stop a madman from sending his own men to die for his near-sighted and black intentions.

"Go! We have little time left," Thorn shouted, and the men scrambled to do as commanded, filing from the great hall to prepare.

Garrick remained behind, striding to Thorn and placing a hand on his shoulder.

"Ye truly mean tae give yerself up tae MacDougal?" he asked, his brows dipped into a vicious V. Garrick had never liked MacDougal, and Thorn knew his friend hated Thorn putting himself in danger, but there was little else either Thorn or Garrick could do about it. Garrick knew that, too.

"Aye. I cannot allow Briar to pay for whatever it is MacDougal thinks I have done."

"Apparently, he thinks you have done something worth all this insanity," Rose grumbled, her arms crossed over her chest. He knew that look, it meant she was displeased and he was bound for a confrontation with her. Usually, he looked forward to their confrontations, because they usually led to quick and brutal coupling, but this time, he knew there would be no pleasure in the end.

"I will go, I will speak with him. Hopefully, he can be reasoned with," Thorn offered, knowing full well that reason had gone the way of the wind with MacDougal. But, for Briar, for his people, he would try. "If all goes well, I will return with her before the sunrise."

Garrick snorted his disbelief but Rose remained silent.

Examining her expression, Thorn noticed there was a determined set to her head, and that her eyes were flickering from dark to light brown as though she were quickly shuffling through one thought after another.

What is she thinking? He would forever be asking that question, but now was not the time for that.

"Rose, I expect you to remain here where it is safe."

Waiting for her absolute refusal, Thorn was thrown when she simply notched her chin and said, "Aye."

Her answer offered little relief.

For the next hour, Thorn focused on his men, their preparations, and his desire not to die. He knew he was walking into a trap, but there was no choice. When he'd become laird, he knew his duty was to his people, to the very point of death. He was ready to die for any one of the MacPhersons and their kin.

But, God, I want to live.

His gaze scoured the great hall, looking for Rose. After the missive had arrived and the plans were set in motion, she'd disappeared, and that made Thorn's wariness bang against him. Where was she? If he was going to his death, he wanted to see her one last time, to press himself into her welcome heat one more time, to visit heaven in her arms one last time.

Garrick's heavy footfalls made Thorn look up from where his hands were fisted in his lap.

"'Tis time, Thorn," he murmured, his head low.

Thorn swallowed the sudden rush of emotion—for his friend and for the reality of what was coming.

"Thank you, for all you have done, my friend," Thorn said, rising to his feet to embrace the man who was more his brother than his head of guard.

"Dinnae thank me yet, ye bastard. Ye still have tae come back. Then, ye can thank me proper, with a feast in my honor."

Chuckling deeply, Thorn slapped Garrick on the back.

Nary twenty minutes later, Thorn rode through the outer bailey gates of Gleneden, his course set for his probable death, and yet...his thoughts were on the woman he was leaving behind.

CHAPTER 16

Getting into Kinlochbern was much easier than Rose had expected, which only made her all the more alert. It was possible that MacDougal's men were focused on the front gate through which Thorn would ride, but what sort of man would leave his rear flank unprotected?

He's mad, and he's arrogant. 'Tis no wonder he thinks himself impervious. The man believed he had Thorn by the bollocks, but the bastard didn't know that those bollocks belonged to Rose and she was determined to protect them. And that meant sneaking into the large keep, finding Briar, and then rescuing the twat. After Briar was secure, Rose would return to rescue Thorn. That was the plan, anyway.

Now, dressed in a plain brown frock she'd snatched from a drying line behind the kitchens, Rose made her way down a corridor she hoped would take her to the upper levels of the castle. Aye, Briar could have been taken to the dungeons, but Rose had a feeling that Briar wasn't simply an innocent casualty of a one-sided family feud. She couldn't explain the feeling, but instinct had never steered her wrong before. There was something about the woman that had always struck Rose wrong, as though she were hiding her true self behind her pretty dresses, her practiced smiles, and her supposed understanding of Thorn's dismissal of their betrothal. If Rose had been dismissed—hell, if any woman were dismissed by the betrothed they had been pining after for decades—she wouldn't have been quite so nice about it.

Pushing aside her thoughts, she continued forward, her feet taking her to the very end of one corridor where she came face to face with a guard in full armor. He was a hulking brute, and smell of sour arse and ale, and he was standing at the bottom of a staircase that wound upward around a central support. She had to get up there.

Thankfully, the smelly brute was asleep on his feet, leaning against the wall with his head thrown back, snoring into the low-hanging ceiling. Rose bit back a snicker then slid by him.

Hurrying upward, she made it to the second floor of the castle. It was semi-dark with flickering candles in sconces, one every six feet. And every six feet was a closed door.

Damn! Finding Briar would take an age at that rate, and Rose didn't have an age. She needed to get to Thorn—the urgency was beating at her, making her skin feel too tight for her bones. She couldn't lose Thorn, he'd come to mean much to her during their short, passionate, feverish love affair.

Is that all it is? An affair—there and then done? She refused to think on it just then, though she knew she would have to.

Soon.

Walking with shuffling movements, as a chambermaid would, Rose stopped to open the door on several rooms, some of which were occupied, but none were occupied with Briar. She slowly, quietly shut the final door in that corridor, and heaved a sigh. She'd looked into five rooms so far on that floor. Cursing to herself she almost missed the noise from the room furthest down the hallway.

Holding her breath, Rose waited for the noise to sound again, and when it did, she grinned. It was the sound of a rabidly unhappy woman.

Briar.

Her hand reaching for a sword she hadn't brought with her—dammit! —she tensed, slowly moving forward. She doubted that Briar was shouting at no one, which meant there was someone in the room with her.

At the door, Rose pressed her ear against it, trying to make out what the woman was going on about.

"MacDougal promised I would want for nothin', and that means if I want a plate o' fresh tarts, I get a plate o' fresh tarts!" she shrilled, and Rose recoiled.

Tarts? The woman was a prisoner, her life hanging by a noose, a noose Thorn would wear, and she was complaining about tarts?

This is not right....

A male's voice answered, but Rose couldn't make out what he was saying.

"When I am lady o' Gleneden, ye will find that I am a vicious enemy, ye daft git, I promise ye that."

Lady of Gleneden? To be the lady, she'd have to marry the laird. But Thorn was laird and he'd broken off their short engagement, hadn't he?

As questions thrust themselves into Rose's mind, the bitch behind the door shrilled again.

"Hurt but no' dead, damn him. MacDougal swore he wouldnae kill Thorn—" Rose couldn't make out what she said next, only sharp mutterings, and then— "Let me out o' here! I want tae be with Thorn! If ye hurt him, I will never forgive ye!"

Slowly, Briar's words formed into a hideous, slimy truth in Rose's mind. Briar MacPherson wasn't in danger, she was a betrayer. She had sided with MacDougal to get what she'd always wanted: Thorn.

Suddenly, all the blood in Rose's body pooled in her feet.

Briar wasn't a prisoner...she was a conspirator. A desperate, grasping, whore of a traitor.

As she stood there, outside the door, listening to Briar and the unknown man mutter back and forth as though hell hadn't descended on their world, Rose sneered diabolically.

Briar would pay for ever crossing a Rees.

Raising a hand, Rose knocked on the door—three loud slams of her fist.

The murmuring immediately stopped. Silence followed. Then, the latch clicked and the door swung open an inch.

Rose grinned up into the face of a man she'd never seen before, but before she was done with him, he'd only ever see her face in his dreams.

"What ye want, wench?" the man growled, scowling down at her.

"I am here to deliver a message," Rose replied, her hands twitching and eager for action, to wrap themselves around the throat of the woman who'd dared wrong someone she loved.

Loved! Love? She *loved* Thorn?

Hell.

"And what message is that?" the man asked, his eyes narrowing at her.

Rose chuckled, a thrill shooting through her.

"Tell her Rose Rees has come to cut out her lying tongue."

With that, a screech sounded behind the man and the man threw the door open, reaching down to draw his sword.

He didn't have time.

Rose pulled her dagger from her waistband, thrusting it into the man's throat, his blood spraying her cheeks with warmth.

Wiping the dagger on the hem of her tunic, Rose slid it back into her waistband and sighed dramatically. Stepping over the man, who was desperately trying to keep his blood from pouring from his neck, Rose met Briar's wide, terrified gaze.

And laughed.

CHAPTER 17

Thorn tossed his horse's reins to an armor-clad man who was glaring at him with such hatred in his eyes that Thorn could feel it, like a dark flame devouring his skin.

Damn.

Raising his arms as a sign he was unarmed, Thorn waited for the two men by the large oak door to come down the stone steps toward him.

"Dubhach MacPherson," one man sneered, "Honestly thought ye'd tuck yer tail n' flee. A coward, just like yer brother."

At mention of Aron, Thorn's body tensed, growing taut to the point his finger joints popped.

"You will not speak of my brother, you swine," Thorn growled, taking a step toward the man who ignorantly continued to grin at Thorn. If Thorn were armed, he would have removed the man's head from his shoulders with a single swing, and he'd enjoy it.

"Let him alone, Francis. MacDougal isnae willin' tae wait until yer done shakin' yer willy at MacPherson," the other man snapped, obviously a higher-ranking guard.

The other man, Francis, grumbled but backed away, allowing Thorn to pass by.

He knew he was walking through the door to his doom, but what choice did he have? Briar didn't deserve to be MacDougal's prisoner, not for something that had nothing to do with her.

She had better be grateful for this!

Damn. He hated that his life was on a perilous edge, that he was placing his hope on a deranged man's sense of mercy.

As he entered the great hall, he noticed that both sides of the large room were lined with people, all staring at him with curiosity, and some with hatred.

Thorn couldn't believe that people with such a dislike of him lived so close to him, his family, his people. What had MacDougal told them, what lies had he spread that had made them all so willing to watch this farce of justice?

Suddenly, that one sliver of his mind that believed this was a good idea disappeared.

Seeing now, the look on Malcolm MacDougal's face, Thorn knew there would be no mercy.

He would die here.

So be it. Squaring his shoulders, he straightened to his full height, refusing to look away, to give the madman before him the satisfaction of seeing him cower. He would never cower, not when he could save a life—even if it wasn't his.

"Dubhach MacPherson, ye have come tae face justice for what ye have done," MacDougal bellowed, already sweating and red-faced.

"And what have I done, MacDougal?" Thorn asked, his voice unwavering.

MacDougal's face deepened to apoplectic purple. "Ye dare deny that ye are responsible for the death o' my boy, my Bruce?" he spat, his fists shaking at his sides.

Thorn lifted a single eyebrow. "Aye, I deny it. I was not there. I had nothing to do with Bruce's death, and you know that. And yet you continue to spread your hate and your poison, unable to face the fact that he is dead, and the one who was responsible is dead. What happened was a tragedy, one that was felt by all. You are not the only one who lost someone that day. So, should I, who lost a brother and a friend, seek vengeance against you? Was it not your river they jumped in to? Could you not have stopped the flow of the water, perhaps slowed it enough for them to struggle to the shore? Could you not have demanded the water level to decrease so their feet could touch the bottom?"

"How dare ye!" MacDougal squealed, but Thorn raised his hand to silence the blubbering fool.

"Nay? 'Tis ridiculous to blame you for your inability to control the river? Is it not just as ridiculous to seek justice against someone who could not control the actions of another, who was not even present during the ill-fated event? And yet, that is what you are doing, that is what you have been panting for for decades." Thorn's blood pounded through his veins, his chest heaving as his emotions surged. "You are a fool, MacDougal, a mad old fool."

The people lining the walls all stared at him, mouths agape, their faces pale. How had they not realized the truth of things before now? They were all fools, dammit!

Without warning, MacDougal screamed, jumping from the dais on which he stood, like a judge presiding over a hellish trial. He reached Thorn in a moment, his mouth twisted, his body trembling in his rage. And yet, Thorn stood still, watching, waiting for the inevitable.

He'd said his piece and now, whatever would come would come.

"Ye will die, and then I will watch as Gleneden burns and the MacPhersons are wiped from existence." His words were loud enough to echo through the large room, bouncing off the walls to slam into Thorn's chest.

"You would kill innocent people?" Thorn demanded, incredulous.

MacDougal roared. "There isnae a single innocent MacPherson. They must all pay!"

Shocked gasps rose up, and the people around them began to murmur. Did they not realize their laird was willing to kill innocents in his quest for unrighteous vengeance? It was what he was doing just then, with Thorn, a man who had done nothing but be born a MacPherson. A man who had already spent twenty-one years of his life, making up for the loss of Lord Owains's heir? He'd sacrificed twenty-one years of time he could have spent with his father, with his mother, a woman who died only two years after Thorn was sent to foster in Wales for a tragedy he had no hand in. But he went willingly because it was the right thing to do, just as it was the right thing to do to sacrifice his life to save Briar.

But he couldn't think about the fate of the other MacPhersons, he needed to focus on the here and now. Perhaps the other MacDougals could sway their laird.

He took a chance to peer from the corner of his eye, seeking any expression that showed horror where there was once hatred. Some were whispering to one another, and some were moving toward the door, turning their backs on the proceedings.

And they thought *him* a coward.

Nay! This cannot happen! 'Tis unfair! Where was the justice for him? He was the Laird MacPherson! How could there be none who would voice outrage for him, or cry out in defense of his innocence?

His jaw muscles tensed, grinding his teeth together until he tasted his own blood. He sucked in a ragged breath, forcing a calm he would never truly feel again.

Nay, it was impossible for him to die that day. He refused to. He would fight with his bare hands, until every one of his bones was broken, until every ounce of his blood stained the stone floors, until his last breath was cast into the heavens.

"I am here, just as you demanded. Release Briar, allow her to return to Gleneden," Thorn ground out, pinning his gaze back on the man who held Thorn's life in his hands.

"I doubt you want that," a familiar voice chirped into the void left by the silence after his demand. Alarm blazed through him as he watched Rose stride into the great hall through a door behind the dais. She was holding a length of rope, and at the end of the rope was a pale-faced Briar, her dark hate-filled eyes glittering with recently shed tears.

MacDougal took one look at Rose and began to chuckle. It was a hideous laugh, one that kicked Thorn in the belly.

"Ye must be the Welsh whore that usurped Briar's position in MacPherson's bed," MacDougal sneered wickedly. MacDougal raised his hand toward where Briar and Rose were standing, his lips curling up once more. "She has done naught but mutter about the 'bitch who stole her Thorn'."

Struck but what MacDougal was saying, Thorn watched as Briar ducked her head, hiding her face from his view. A sick tingling began in the back of his throat.

"What have you done, Briar?" he ground out.

Rose answered for her, "She betrayed you. She told me all about how she came to MacDougal, promising to get you here so that MacDougal could have his revenge. Idiot actually believed that MacDougal only meant to torture you a little, leaving you alive so she could come to your side, playing the loving and attentive woman you wronged. You would be grateful, you would cast me aside, and she would finally have you all to herself."

Dumbfounded, Thorn could only stare at Rose as her announcement rang in his ears.

"That cannot be true," he murmured, anger slowly boiling within him. "What have you done, Briar?" he demanded again.

Again MacDougal chuckled. "What does it matter? It worked, did it no? And now ye are here, and so is the woman ye have been waitin' yer whole life tae marry. Och, aye, I ken that she is Rose MacDeargh, long-lost daughter of Angus MacDeargh, thought dead for these twenty-one years. Not only does she look just like her dear da, she has a head o' fire, just like her mother. Also, it was easy enough tae uncover the truth. Ye really shouldnae asked so many questions in the village. They are gossipers, the lot o' them."

As MacDougal was speaking, a tall, blonde stranger edged along the room, sticking to the shadows until he came up, right behind Rose. The man's striking sea green eyes shone with something akin to terrible joy.

Thorn opened his mouth to yell, to warn Rose, but it was too late. The man reached out, throwing his arms around Rose, pinning her arms to her sides. The dagger she'd been holding fell to the floor with a clang.

"God dammit, no!"

He needed to get to her, to save her, but his feet wouldn't move. Overwhelming fear held him in place, fear for himself, fear for his people, even fear for the treasonous Briar, but most of all, he feared for Rose. If he moved, the man holding her could easily end her life. Right before his eyes.

Never in his life had he felt so helpless. Rose was caught, and there wasn't anything Thorn could do to save her.

Hold on, my love...

CHAPTER 18

Twisting to get a better look at the dog holding her, she cursed. The bloody bastard! She would kill him the first chance she got. Rose struggled against the man's hold, kicking her heel back to connect with his shins, but he maneuvered, easily avoiding the hit.

"Easy, wench!" the bastard barked, and Rose bit back the urge to bend down and take a bite out of the arm wound around her chest.

Across the room, MacDougal threw his head back and laughed into the ceiling, his maniacal gaze dancing.

"'Tis beautiful tae see justice comin' from all sides, is it no, MacPherson? Ye will die here, I promise ye that, but first, I think ye should watch yer woman die, slow 'n painful."

Thorn roared, breaking free of the invisible barrier that had held him in place throughout the disgusting show of madness. In two strides, MacDougal's men had drawn their swords, holding them to MacPherson's throat.

"Nay! Rose!" Thorn bellowed, looking to force his way through despite the blade points at his neck, but two other men appeared, pulling his arms behind his back. Thorn struggled, and Rose's heart fell into the pit of her stomach.

If Thorn died here, she would kill MacDougal herself. Then she'd deal with the bastard behind her now, cutting his nose from his pretty face.

"Now, now, MacPherson. Is that any way tae greet my honored guest? He is all the way from Wales, and I was able tae secure his services. I am sure ye have heard o' his family—a lot o' savages, and this one is the most vicious. Said tae be the best torture master in Europe, and I paid him tae be here, just in case I had need o' him." MacDougal grinned. "Lucky that, aye?"

Bile flooded Rose's mouth and she turned to glare at the man behind her.

In Welsh she grated, "Have you no pride?"

He pinned her with a smile utterly free of guilt. "What of you, Cousin? When did you start bedding nobility, and Scottish nobility at that?"

Rose stiffened at Thorn's gasp, and when she turned to face him, there was a look of disbelief on his face.

It hit her then; he'd lived in Wales, no doubt he'd learned to speak Welsh, which meant that he'd just heard and understood her exchange.

"What sort of trouble have you gotten yourself into, Red?" her cousin asked, bending low to whisper into her ear. Though he spoke in Welsh, it was best that MacDougal not realize their familiar connection, at least not yet.

"Rees," MacDougal called, "Ye will get yer chance at her shortly, but nae before I am finished with her lover."

"Rees?" Thorn snapped. "You are a *Rees*?"

"Lucian Rees," her cousin announced, far too cheerfully for the situation. If he weren't holding her, she had no doubt he would have offered a pretty curtsey.

Rose tossed Thorn a look that told him to remain silent, and he caught the look, pinching his lips together to keep from saying anything else that could ruin whatever plan her cousin was, even now, conjuring to get them the hell out of there alive.

Still speaking in Welsh, Rose murmured, "What are you doing in Kinloch Rannoch?"

Lucian puffed an annoyed breath against her cheek.

"What do you think? That you could run off without one of us chasing after you? We could not just leave you to your own devices, especially since you have become so...restless."

Restless? Oh, aye. She'd always felt apart from the other Rees, knowing she wasn't blood-tied to any of them, but it wasn't until Robbie, one of the long-lost Rees, found them that Rose began to wonder what it would be like to find her own family. It had eaten away at her, day by day, until sex and booze were the only things to take the edge off the ache that drowned her.

And now, she knew the answers, she knew where she came from, she knew where she belonged. She belonged with Dubhach MacPherson.

So why are you fighting him? Why can you not let him be what you want, what you need?

Because she was terrified! If she let Thorn in past the wall she'd built around her heart, how could she guard herself against the hurt that would come if he, too, left her, just as her father and mother had? Nay, they had no choice in the matter, but that hadn't stopped the anguish from souring many of her relationships over the years.

Lucian's embrace loosened, and Rose leaned back into him, conscious of how it would look to anyone watching them. It would appear that she was weakening, and giving in, falling into her captor's hold. In reality...she just missed her cousin. She'd forgotten how comforting his embrace was, how warm and welcoming he was—when he wanted to be.

"The day after you disappeared, Burgess at the Bearded Lady told me about how you'd seemed keen on whatever the MacGuilliams were telling you. It did not take much to discover you had gone north to find your family. So, we came north as well."

"We? You brought Lucia with you?" Rose asked, knowing full

well that wherever one twin went, the other went. They were co-captains of the smuggling sloop, The *Seren Mor*.

"Aye. She has the *Seren Mor* anchored in the loch not far from here."

"But what are you doing with MacDougal? The man is blood hungry." That was an understatement, but now wasn't the time to give Lucian a list of all the lunatic had said and done.

Lucian shrugged carelessly. "When we did not find you immediately, Lucia figured it was a good time for one of us to make some business connections in Scotland, those that aren't already allied with the Scots, the Scourge of Scotia. She remained with the crew and I ducked into the first inn I could find. The men there were discussing MacDougal and how he was looking for a specialist, and I knew I had found something to keep me entertained."

Rose snorted, which made MacDougal turn his attention back to her.

"What do ye find so humorous, wench?" he inquired, his voice deadly calm.

Damn.

"Worry not, Cousin. I have a plan," Lucian said aloud, still in Welsh, his voice carrying to Thorn whose eyes widened in understanding.

Good. Lucian had a plan. Now, to survive whatever plan that was so she could tell Thorn she loved him.

In English, Lucian announced, "The wench was begging for her life. I merely offered her a chance to save it by sucking me dry."

Rose snorted again, rolling her eyes. She would definitely make the bastard pay for such disgusting effrontery.

Thorn narrowed his eyes at Lucian but MacDougal cackled.

"Ye've the bollocks of a giant, Rees," he said, which only made Lucian chuckle into Rose's back. The arse was enjoying this far too much.

"What is this plan of yours?" she asked, her words a sharp hiss.

Lucian's hand moved toward her back where she felt a tugging on her waistband, then he slid his hand around her middle once more. "I have just slipped my favorite stiletto into your skirts, Cousin. Do not lose it. When it happens, it will happen fast, so be ready."

Beneath her breath she asked, "When *what* happens?"

She asked too late. Four men she recognized as part of Lucian's crew, slid up alongside the guards flanking the dais. There were seven guards in total, which were good odds, really. They'd had worse.

"My Lord MacDougal," Lucian began, speaking loud enough for all the gawkers to hear. "I believe there has been a misunderstanding."

MacDougal's face hardened, his thick brows flattening.

"How so, Rees?" He turned away from Thorn and the men holding him.

Rose watched as Lucian gave the men on the right a slight nod, which was a signal easy enough for any Rees to read. Those men edged around the room, through the crowd, until they were within striking distance of the men with their God damn hands on her man.

"When you secured my services, you said I would be torturing a man guilty of a heinous crime against your family."

MacDougal spat. "He is!"

Lucian shook his head. "That is not what I gathered from his rather persuasive speech. Control the river, indeed." He snickered.

"What are ye about, Rees?" MacDougal snapped, moving toward Lucian who stiffened against Rose's back. He dropped his arms from around her and stepped up beside her.

"I may be a smuggler, MacDougal, but I am not a monster. I will not hurt an innocent man, and I certainly will not hurt a woman—innocent or not." He winked down at Rose who screwed up her face in a scowl.

Growling like a rabid animal, MacDougal raised his fist into the air. "If ye willnae help me find justice, I will do it myself!" He snapped his head around and yelled, "Take them all!"

With another quick nod, Lucian kicked into action, leaping over the table on the dais to land on the other side. Lord, she'd forgotten how agile the man was. Once on the other side, Lucian pulled his sword from his scabbard, placing the point directly against MacDougal's Adam's apple.

It had happened so quickly, Rose hadn't had time to even realize what was going on, and it hadn't helped that, once Lucian jumped the table, her focus had turned back to Thorn. He was struggling against the hold of the men around him, but even that didn't last long.

The *Seren Mor* crew moved in, their sword points at the throats of the guards handling Thorn.

The guards dropped their hands from him as if he were on fire.

In a blink, Thorn was across the room, standing before her, his dark eyes roving over her. Before she could say anything, his mouth descended on hers, taking her lips with a hunger that matched hers. His hands cupping her face, he deepened the kiss, nipping then licking, tasting then groaning. It wasn't until someone in the room coughed that Rose remembered where they were and what was happening.

She pulled back, her breath catching on a shudder.

"Are you alright? Are you hurt?" he asked, his voice husky.

"Lucian would not hurt me," she replied. "I am his favorite cousin."

"Cousin!" MacDougal bellowed, obviously having heard what she'd said.

Lucian chuckled, nodding. "Aye. Here I thought you had met my darling Rose."

Snorting MacDougal shook his head. "She isnae a Rees, she's a MacDeargh."

"Aye, I am that, too," she admitted, smiling. She couldn't believe how good it felt to finally admit that, and it didn't bother her in the least that, in admitting who she really was, she was also admitting to being Thorn's betrothed. Because that's what she wanted to be, more than anything.

Around them, the room filled with murmurs, hushed voices rising and falling as the reality of what was going on began to dawn on the onlookers.

Thorn gazed out among those gathered and sighed. Rose could see a flash of sadness in his eyes before it was pushed aside by a determination she had grown fond of.

"Malcolm MacDougal, what you have done here today is so far beyond criminal that you must be held accountable. You have conspired, manipulated, lied, and threatened to kill those I love."

Love? That one word stuck out over all the others. Was he speaking about her? Searching his face, she saw it—the blaze of hot, deep, breathtaking emotion. For her.

"As the MacPherson, I cannot let this stand. In deciding to kill innocent people, you have given your people over to be murderers. You would have them slit the throats of those they sit with in church and make merry with in the market. You have pitted family against family, friend against friend, and you have shown no signs of remorse for what you have done, nor shame for what you planned to do."

Unable to speak with the sharp point of Lucian's blade at his throat, MacDougal only growled, his eyes glittering with hatred. His nostrils flapped like the ears of an ewe, and the whole of his rotund body shook.

But then, his wrathful glare turned upward, into a sickening smile as the sounds of running, booted feet rose over the din. Moments later, two lines of armed men stormed into the room—twenty in total.

Thorn cursed beneath his breath, Rose snatched the stiletto from her skirts, holding it before her in preparation for battle. But Lucian heaved a dramatic sigh.

"Release him!" the largest of the men demanded.

As Rose studied the newcomer, something tickled the back of her mind. It took several moments for that tickling to turn into solid thought.

The man looked far too much like that madman MacDougal.

CHAPTER 19

Thorn sucked in a breath, forcing his chest to move normally despite the way his heart was banging against his ribs in a frantic need to get Rose to safety.

She can take care of herself, which she has proven over and over. And her cousin was there as well. Hell, Thorn never considered that he would meet another Rees, especially under the present circumstances.

"I said, release him, MacPherson!" Barton bellowed, his face contorted into a look too much like his father's.

"Nay. You are a fool to follow him, Barton, knowing full well the evil he had perpetrated on me and my people. People who have only ever shown hospitality and good to you and yours," Thorn remarked, his brows furrowed in a disappointed grimace.

Lucian Rees dropped his sword from MacDougal's neck but only so he could move behind MacDougal and slip an arm around his throat. It was a submission hold if Thorn ever saw one. It allowed Lucian to hold on to the man without putting his back to the room, and it allowed him use of his sword, if need be.

Without Lucian's sword at his throat, MacDougal opened his

mouth, and hate came out.

"Damn ye, MacPherson! Ye think tae turn my son against me? Ye dare tae try and take another son from me?"

"I did not take your first son from you, MacDougal, and this anger and venom must end here, for the sake of your family and mine."

MacDougal spat, Barton flinching at his father's action.

"Kill them all! Kill them! Kill! Kill!" MacDougal's voice rose until it was shrill enough to grate against the heart beating in Thorn's chest.

Turning to stare at Barton, Thorn watched as several emotions passed over his face. The final expression offered Thorn hope.

Regret.

"Father, time has come tae put the tragedy o' the past behind us," Barton implored, sheathing his sword. His men followed suit, until the only ones brandishing weapons were him, Lucian, and Lucian's men. Aye, Rose was also armed, but there was a queer expression on her face that made Thorn wonder at what she was thinking. The stiletto in her hand trembled. "Thorn MacPherson had nae part in Bruce's death, aye, the lad who did is also dead. Hurtin' innocent people willnae bring Bruce back tae ye."

"I willnae let this die, no until every last MacPherson has paid for Bruce's death!" MacDougal continued, this time struggling against Lucian's hold.

Finally, Lucian leaned in, kissing MacDougal on the cheek. Startled, MacDougal's mouth slammed shut.

"There now, why not keep your mouth that way, lest I cut your tongue from your mouth. Better yet, I will cut your belly open and watch you try to collect your guts."

Horrified gasps filled the air.

"Ye wouldnae," MacDougal dared.

"Oh, I would. I said I would not kill the *innocent*. You are far from that my mad, bloodthirsty friend."

Thorn grunted at the term "friend" but held his tongue.

His focus pinned to the man whose face had turned vermillion with unuttered rage, Thorn allowed the slow burning sense of relief to settle on him. Could it be that this was very nearly over? Could he walk out of Kinlochbern with his head and his woman? Was the bloody, one-sided feud finally at an end?

"What have you, Barton MacDougal? Your father is not fit to remain as head of the MacDougal clan—you know it, they all know it...." He raised his arms, spreading them out to indicate those of the gawking audience who had stayed throughout the horrendous confrontation. "You are a man of loyalty, and you were once a man of honor—"

"I still am, MacPherson. Never doubt that," Barton proclaimed, throwing his shoulders back to push out his chest. "And...I will take care o' my da."

MacDougal opened his mouth to speak but Lucian tightened his hold around the man's neck.

"I will see that he never threatens ye again. Ye have my word on it."

At those words, and the look of utter sincerity on Barton's face, Thorn nearly toppled where he stood, the weight of all he had endured lifting from his body. Rose turned to him, then, her eyes bright with unshed tears, and his heart soared. Were those tears for him?

Throwing his arms around her, he pulled her into his chest, kissing every inch of her beautiful face before finally settling where he wanted to be the most. He took her mouth, savoring her cry of joy. Unfortunately, there was neither the time nor place to truly express what he felt for the woman in his embrace. He broke off their kiss, peering down into her upturned face. He groaned at the haziness in her eyes and the swollen pink of her lips.

"We will continue this conversation once we have returned home," he drawled, his voice deep, raspy.

She blinked, her eyes focusing. "Home," she repeated before a slow, glorious smile broke over her face. "Aye, home."

Lucian relinquished the detainment of MacDougal to two of Barton's men, and as they dragged him, screaming and spitting, from the great hall, Barton's face fell, his shoulders drooping.

"I knew this was comin', I could see the madness in his eyes, but I wanted tae believe he wouldnae go this far." Barton turned to Thorn, offering him his hand. Thorn took it, holding it tightly. "I am truly sorry for all my da has done in his misplaced quest for revenge. I shouldnae let it get this far. I shouldnae followed orders blindly...."

"We are all guilty of allowing love to blind us, Barton. I wanted to believe that my brother was an innocent, that he did not mean to end the life of two lads. But...I realize now, he took his own life because he knew what he had done. He knew that his decisions cost lives." Thorn dropped Barton's hand, his lips lifting into a sad half smile. "At least you were able to stop your da before *he* acted on *his* decisions."

They parted ways then, Thorn's group leaving Kinlochbern and her horrified people behind as they traveled the fifteen miles back to Gleneden. Lucian Rees embraced Rose, promising her he would come to see her the next day, once he and his men had drunk their fill at the inn.

Once in Thorn's study, where Thorn had hoped to kiss Rose until she was panting for him to take her to bed, Rose began to pace instead.

"I will find her, and I will shave her head," Rose grumbled, her temper smoldering over Briar's betrayal and subsequent escape. She'd slipped from the great hall after Lucian had taken hold of MacDougal, but Thorn wasn't worried about her.

"I doubt she will ever show her face at Gleneden again, Little Rose, and if she does—"

"If she does, I will shave her head *and* gouge out her eyes!" Rose ground out, vehemently. Lord, he was glad he was not on the receiving end of Rose's displeasure.

"If she does," Thorn tried again, "she will be tried in a court of justice for lying and risking the life of her laird, and her laird's beloved."

Rose's mouth dropped open, her eyes wide, as Thorn's words pushed through the murderous haze.

"That is the second time today you mentioned love," she intoned, planting her hands on her hips. She'd removed the blood-stained maid's frock she'd worn at Kinlochbern and was, once again, in a loose linen shirt and her black leather breeches. "What have you to tell me, Dubhach?"

He strode to her, wrapping his arms around her and placing his hands against the small of her back. She fit him perfectly.

"I have to tell you that I love you. I have loved you since I saw you wearing exactly this, standing in my great hall, with five of my beaten men around you. I knew right then that my life would never be the same, and I was lost utterly when I realized you were meant to be mine all along, Rose MacDeargh."

Rose couldn't stop smiling even if she sewed her lips together.

The man she loved just told her he loved her, too. The day had been long, and some events were still coming into focus in her thoughts, but in that moment, she didn't care about any of that. She only cared that she and Thorn were alive, they were together, and he loved her.

"Have you anything to tell me, Rose?" Thorn prodded, his eyebrows wiggling.

She giggled then leaned in winding her arms around his neck to pull his head down.

Their eyes met, his dark eyes fathomless and yet bright.

"Aye, I have something to tell you..." she began, teasing him with a long pause. "I came to Kinloch Rannoch looking for the truth about the family I had lost. I did not know that I would find a new family."

Rose could feel Thorn's chest expand just before he held his breath.

"I did not know I would find a man I hoped to be worthy of, a man who was strong, brave, and willing to give up his life for his people—even though the people in question were lying scheming bitches!" Sucking in a breath, she began again. "I did not know I would find something I had always wanted: love."

Thorn let out his breath slowly, his gaze never leaving hers.

"What do you mean?" he asked, his voice heavy.

"I mean that I love you, *Thorny*, and I don't want to be your betrothed all that long because being your wife sounds better."

With a loud, exuberant whoop, Thorn hauled her into him, picking her up off the ground to swing her around. She laughed heartily; her soul finally alight with true happiness. After a moment, Thorn stopped, setting her on her feet.

"What about Lucian and the other Rees?"

She had been thinking on that for several days now, and she'd come to a decision even before the gorgeous beast before her told her he loved her.

"They will do fine without me. I was only ever the gatherer of information, which is a job anyone of them can do."

"Surely you are not as replaceable as that," Thorn argued.

She chuckled. "Having experienced the horrors of a shipwreck, I was never one to board a ship without first being disgustingly drunk. What good is a smuggler who can't sail without more whiskey than blood in their veins?"

It was Thorn's turn to chuckle. "I see. So...you will not mind being land-locked at Gleneden?"

Rose pressed a soft kiss to his mouth, smiling into him.

"As long as I am with you."

"You are to be a rebellious Rees, then," Thorn joked, smirking.

"Nay, I have always been rebellious. 'Tis nothing new."

"Rebellious Rose Rees, my love," he murmured into her lips, kissing her as though her breath gave him life.

When they broke their kiss long moments later, Rose finally replied, "Rebellious Rose MacPherson, if you please."

ABOUT THE AUTHOR

Rosamund Winchester is a determined and overwhelmed mother of four children. If she didn't have writing to focus on, she'd spend all day staring into space and pondering the mysteries of the universe.

Rosamund writes emotional, thrilling, heart-pounding historical romance that draws the reader into the adventure, the passion, and the happily ever after. Rosamund also writes sweet historical romance as Lynn Winchester, so she offers books for all romance lovers.

When Rosamund isn't writing sexy historical romance, or sweet historical romance as Lynn Winchester, she is reading whatever she is in the mood for, or watching crime shows on Discovery ID.

OTHER BOOKS BY ROSAMUND WINCHESTER

The Men of Blood Series

Dark Medieval Romance

The Blood and the Bloom

The Fire and the Sword

The Ravishing Rees Series

Swashbuckling Pirate Romance

The Beast of Blades

www.ingramcontent.com/pod-product-compliance
Ingram Content Group UK Ltd.
Pitfield, Milton Keynes, MK11 3LW, UK
UKHW041640190726
13854UKWH00006B/2611

9 798761 573987